"What the  you're doing

Jezebel spun toward the [...] and fell smack on her behind in the mud.

Backlit by the rising sun's rays, a powerful, menacing frame towered over her. "Get off my property." The man's voice was guttural and fierce.

She shaded her eyes as she struggled to her feet—

And stared straight into the furious face of the man she most did not want to see.

He advanced on her. "You're trespassing. Beat it."

She backed into the rock edging and lost her footing again. She grappled for something, anything, to catch her—

Instead, Gamble did.

The touch of this angry stranger had nothing in common with the eager, bone-melting caresses of the night before or the man who'd leaped to her rescue. He gripped her arms so tightly she knew she'd bruise.

"I'll give you thirty seconds. Then I'm calling the sheriff." He squeezed harder, his face blazing with contempt. "I'll never sell this house to you. Got that?"

Dear Reader,

Those of you who read my Signature Select Saga novel, *Mercy,* probably didn't pick out Gamble Smith for a likely character to be the hero of his own book.

Welcome to the club.

I always felt that there was much more to his complicated relationship with Kat Gerard than was visible on the surface, but that novel wasn't the place for me to find out what drove him.

I never forgot Gamble, however, or quit being curious about what made him tick. The answer to his seemingly cavalier treatment of Kat, though, surprised me just as much as it may surprise you. I hope you'll find in him a man both to admire and to love, as I have.

Jezebel Hart is, on the surface, a very unlikely match for Gamble, but she sure was a lot of fun to write! She's a walking, talking lesson that family can be found in unlikely places and have ties every bit as strong as blood.

I hope you'll enjoy meeting both a close-knit and loving family bound by blood and another, odder family knit together by a woman with a heart big enough to heal a man who thought love was done with him.

It's always a special joy to hear from you. You can reach me by post at P.O. Box 3000 #79, Georgetown, TX 78627 or via my Web site, www.jeanbrashear.com, or Harlequin's Web site, www.eHarlequin.com.

Thank you for allowing me to come into your lives and share my stories. It's an honor and a great pleasure to do so.

All best wishes,

Jean

SWEET MERCY
Jean Brashear

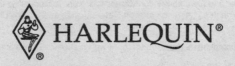

HARLEQUIN®

TORONTO • NEW YORK • LONDON
AMSTERDAM • PARIS • SYDNEY • HAMBURG
STOCKHOLM • ATHENS • TOKYO • MILAN • MADRID
PRAGUE • WARSAW • BUDAPEST • AUCKLAND

ISBN 0-373-71339-8

SWEET MERCY

www.eHarlequin.com

Printed in U.S.A.

Books by Jean Brashear

HARLEQUIN SUPERROMANCE
1071–WHAT THE HEART WANTS
1105–THE HEALER
1142–THE GOOD DAUGHTER
1190–A REAL HERO
1219–MOST WANTED
1251–COMING HOME
1267–FORGIVENESS

SIGNATURE SELECT SAGA
MERCY

For Ercel, whose existence is the sweetest mercy
life has ever granted to me

PROLOGUE

Manhattan

THE BAGS OF GROCERIES hit the floor with a thud.

Gamble Smith launched himself from the mattress. Yanked on his jeans. Faced Kat Gerard's stricken eyes.

"You said it was over." Another woman's plaintive voice from his bed.

Gamble ignored her. Steeled himself to endure whatever would happen. He had to remind Kat— remind himself—of their terms. Of what he could never give her.

But even *his* desiccated heart was apparently capable of too much emotion.

Kat stirred, finally, from the shocked and frozen silence, her fierce beauty gone slack. She grabbed the soul-baring portrait of herself from his easel. Raced back down the stairs from his loft.

He charged after her, scarcely caught her before she got to the street.

She bared her teeth. "I'll smash it on the pole if you don't let me go."

He dropped her arm, but not to save his work. She deserved a chance to ream him.

Her look did it for her. At last, she spoke. "A lie, all of it?"

He cautioned himself to hold fast. "I told you I don't have room in my life for you."

"You did." Her expression was desolate. "More the fool me that I didn't listen."

Then sour laughter erupted from her chest. "It ought to be funny, you know? I'm the one who decides when it's over, the one who discards. It's been that way for years. There are many who'd say this is my just desserts."

"Kat—" Guilt flickered. And pity. He reached for her.

She recoiled as if from a leper.

He dropped his hand. "It went too far. I can't—" He exhaled. "You made me feel things I can't afford."

"Why not? Just answer me that. Surely you owe me as much."

With the heels of his hands, he rubbed his eyes, then dropped the bomb.

"Because I'm married."

A stunned instant later, Kat slapped him hard, then stared at the imprint on his cheek.

"I'm not giving this back," she said of the painting he'd done of her, his finest work yet.

"It's yours," he said, his voice raw. It was the least he could do; the show she'd mounted in her Chelsea gallery had brought him his first taste of fame.

Too bad the flavor of success was a poor substitute for the sweetness of Charlotte's kiss. The glory of her love. "Kat…"

"No." She dodged his attempt to soothe. "Where is she?"

"Back in Texas."

"You bastard. What the hell are you doing in New York?"

"It's complicated." He glanced away. "I couldn't paint there. I couldn't breathe." *Didn't want to live.*

"So you just walk out, do you? Simply forget her?"

"No," he said, voice as hollow as his heart. "I don't forget."

"Go home, Gamble." Awkwardly, she dashed tears with one hand—fearless Kat, who never, ever wept. Then she gathered herself to leave.

"Kat." Gamble's hoarse timbre stopped her. "Find someone who deserves you. Quit screwing around." He pointed to the painting. "Let her live. She deserves better."

Kat didn't respond. Without another word, she

departed slowly, her proud, graceful bearing diminished.

Leaving him the only way he knew to be.

Alone.

He watched her go. And bled. That Kat was the one who'd pursued him—relentlessly, in fact, until he'd finally caved—didn't matter. He should have resisted harder, but even the hollow man he'd become sometimes craved human connection.

Instead of a simple scratch to an itch they'd both intended, however, Kat had come too close to a heart that was already given.

Even if the woman who owned it had been dead for two years.

CHAPTER ONE

One month later

IN HIS DREAMS, *she was always there in the cottage he'd built for her, every stick and brick a testament to love.*

Her face was a song, her smile the grace note. A waterfall of golden hair spilled halfway down her back; the soft hazel eyes had been his lodestone since he was ten and she was eight. He'd understood then that his purpose in life was to protect her.

But he hadn't counted on needing to safeguard her from herself. From her fierce desire to bear his child, despite the danger the doctors had predicted.

Gamble Smith stirred on the lumpy mattress. Whipped his head from side to side, seeking the path back to heaven. One more sight of Charlotte, ensconced in the swing on the wide porch she'd wanted. Another moment to sit with her and rock while they examined the dogwoods he'd planted as saplings. Or wander through the fragrant rose beds he'd dug around the back, now bursting with color.

"Unhh— Don't go," he begged her. *Stay this time.*

Charlotte rose, one hand tenderly pressed to the gentle mound he had cursed. The saddest eyes in the world begged his understanding. With her other hand, she blew him a kiss, just like on that last day. He'd left her only long enough to retrieve a surprise—the crib he'd made as a peace offering.

But he'd returned too late. Always too late. She lay where she'd collapsed when the clot had hit her lung, a porcelain angel, on the porch where she'd waved goodbye to him with a promise.

That she would be fine. That he should have faith.

That love would be enough.

Lies, all lies.

Charlotte was gone, leaving behind her a man, a life, a dream.

Without a heart.

Sirens crashed into his restless slumber.

"Charlotte—" Gamble jerked upright and groped the mattress beside him. "Charlotte, I'm—" *Sorry.*

The screech of tires. The swoosh of bus air brakes. A roar of city traffic, not the lazy rustling of East Texas pines.

His head sank into his hands. He was still in New York.

He wrenched himself from the mattress, pulled on his jeans and sought escape in his work.

FOR THE FIRST few breaths of the morning, he thought maybe he could finally do it: paint that portrait of Charlotte he'd promised her years ago, after he'd stored away his brushes and pigments. Turned to painting houses to pay the endless medical bills required by an enlarged heart, weak and pumping abnormally.

But no matter how many times he rendered other women with bold strokes, his hands trembled as soon as he attempted the only project he really cared about: the picture Charlotte had wanted from him. She'd grieved over the sacrifice he'd had to make of his art; he never had. Nothing, not even the work that sustained his soul, had meant as much to him as she did.

The buzzer squawked downstairs. Gamble wiped his hands on a cloth and considered ignoring it.

Then he remembered that it wouldn't be Kat anymore. As the owner of the gallery with first rights to his work, she'd expressed, often and loudly, her fury that he refused to have a phone in this derelict warehouse that was both home and studio, requiring that she seek him out when she needed to contact him.

But he hadn't seen Kat in a month. The necessary correspondence had been conducted via messenger and limited to crisp sentences. Checks delivered, paintings surrendered, all into the hands of intermediaries.

Just business. Simple commerce.

As he and Kat should have done all along. And if he missed the spice she had brought into his gray days, well, it was no more than he'd earned.

Anyway, Kat was engaged now, to a far better man. One who deserved her.

While Gamble was painting as if he were a man possessed, suddenly the toast of the town. He ate when he remembered and slept when he could no longer hold a brush. And somewhere in the haze of it, he thought he recalled getting a letter from his brother, Levi, that someone had made an offer to buy his cottage.

Charlotte's cottage.

Where Gamble couldn't bear to live.

When he'd walked away from Three Pines, Texas, he'd left everything and everyone behind. Only twice in the year he'd been gone had the loneliness forced him to call home, and when he had, his family's understanding had nearly broken his resolve.

But he couldn't stay in Three Pines, where Charlotte's memory was in the very air he breathed.

The buzzer insisted.

"All right, all right." He threw up his hands. He wasn't getting anything done anyway. Down the stairs he went.

"Yeah?"

"Messenger."

He opened the door. "Who is it from?"

"No idea." In a rush as all New Yorkers were, the kid shoved an envelope at him and held out a palm for the tip.

"Oh." Gamble patted the pockets of his paint-smeared jeans, unearthed a couple of ones. "This enough?" Kat had harangued him to set up a proper bank account. He still sent all but the bare minimum he needed back to Three Pines. He wasn't here for money; he was in New York to honor a vow. To find a reason to keep going.

"Whatever." The messenger's scowl said Gamble could have done better, but he simply waved and left.

Gamble stood in the open doorway and stared at the envelope in his hand. Finally, he opened it and read.

This isn't New York. Buyers aren't waiting around every corner. You wanted to give me your power of attorney, but I'm not signing these papers for you, Gamble, and I'm not mailing them to you, either. Mom misses you; we all do. If you're ready to sell the cottage, then come back and prove it.

Gamble was already shaking his head in annoyance when he scanned down to the bottom of the page.

P.S. Mom's birthday is in two days, and yes, the painting you did for her arrived in good shape, but I'm holding it hostage until we see your ugly face.

Gamble chuckled at his elder brother's taunt. He sighed and dropped his head. Rubbed the bridge of his nose and wished that Levi would leave him the hell alone, knowing there wasn't a chance that would happen. The Smith clan stuck like glue.

He rolled his shoulders, tried out a series of arguments.

Then trod back up the stairs to pack.

Three Pines, Texas

"I HEARD THAT, LOUIE." Jezebel Hart paused in the act of clearing a table of beer mugs and nudged the jar she kept for fines in her favorite customer's direction.

"You couldn't have. The damn jukebox is so loud a body can't hear himself think."

Jezebel lifted one eyebrow. "That'll be three dollars now."

Along the bar rose a chorus of snickers and hoots.

Louie slapped one hand on the darkened wood. "Bossy—" he managed to stifle the curse word, if just barely "—woman."

"Gimme." She picked up his mug and wiped the bar beneath it. "It's for a good cause." From the proceeds of her No Profanity jar, she'd been able to fund a community Christmas dinner for all those facing the meal alone. The first swear word by each person, customer or staff, was a dollar; succeeding offenses in a given night doubled the previous amount. Refuse to pay, and you were banned from the premises for a week.

Sure, they'd grumbled when she'd instituted it last October, Louie loudest of all, but he'd eaten every bite of that Christmas dinner and come back for seconds.

"No way to run a bar," Louie muttered the whole time he was digging out his wallet.

Jezebel leaned closer, just in case she could catch one more slip of his tongue.

Louie slapped three bills on the ancient oak. "Don't see why Skeeter had to go and leave us with a fascist."

They grinned at each other.

With a name like Jezebel and exotic dancing in her checkered past, she figured that running a bar was about as much peril as her mortal soul could afford. She was out to balance the scales.

She resumed cleaning a table. Bobby Redstone ambled up behind her. "Jezebel, baby—"

She recoiled from the assault of whiskey fumes. "Last call for you, sugar." She smiled. "But there's some coffee with your name on it."

"Baby, I'm dyin' for love of you." He made a sloppy grab for her long curly hair. "C'mere. You kiss me now."

She glanced over at Darrell Garrett, her cook, bartender and bouncer—all six foot five and three hundred pounds of him—and shook her head to restrain him. At five-ten, she was no pushover herself. She'd been dodging male hands since her abundant curves seemed to spring full-blown at fourteen.

She slipped an arm around Bobby's waist. "I can't risk Louie getting jealous—you know that. No telling what that man might do. Break my heart if he messed up your pretty face."

Drunk as he was, even Bobby got the joke. Louie was near eighty if he was a day, about five-six and scrawny as a hen ready for the cookpot.

"No fair, Jezebel. Ever' damn night, I got to look at the most beautiful woman in the world and can't do nuthin' about it. Who you savin' it for, baby?" He tried to nuzzle her neck.

"My heart belongs to Louie. If he won't have me, I'm done with romance." Her dancer's legs performed a smooth sidestep. Before he could register what had happened, she'd seated him in a booth and was on her way to procure coffee.

"You are too good, girl," Darrell murmured. "If I had moves like that, I'd be in the NFL today."

She patted his arm and smiled. "Shirley appears to like your moves just fine. Baby managing more than two hours at a time yet?"

His shoulders slumped. "Don't remind me."

"Sleep in tomorrow. I'll meet the beer truck."

"Won't help. The other kids have to get up for school."

She noted the clock. "They're already in bed, right?"

"Good Lord willin'."

"Wish I could keep them for you, so you and Shirley could sleep. Maybe you can nap after they leave."

His shoulder-length dreadlocks shook with his laughter. "Girl, I was sure you were crazy. I just didn't realize how much."

"I love your kids."

"And they adore you. But even if you had room back there in that glorified storage space you call an apartment, exactly when do you plan to get some rest yourself? You're already working twenty hours a day, best I can tell, between running this place and caring for Skeeter." He frowned. "It wouldn't kill you to let someone help you for a change."

She'd been on her own since she was thirteen;

doing for herself was a hard habit to break. "I have to make this place succeed. Skeeter's counting on me."

Skeeter Owens was the closest thing to a grandfather Jezebel had ever had. They'd met in Reno, where he'd gone for a busman's holiday to gamble; she'd been a cocktail waitress. He'd discouraged a too-ardent patron, and they'd conversed through the rest of the evening as she served his table. He'd given her a tip too big for her to turn down, no matter what strings might be attached. She'd never resorted to selling her body, but there had been lean, scary days in her past when that one last step was all that was left.

But the only thing Skeeter wanted was to buy her breakfast and talk. Before she noticed, she'd spilled out more of her life story than she'd ever shared with a soul: orphaned by a fire at five, removed from her junkie aunt at eight, a chronic runaway from foster homes. He'd done the same, telling her about the kids he'd never had and the wife he'd lost a few years before. About the bar that kept him going. They parted with an agreement to write and an invitation from him if she was ever anywhere near Three Pines, Texas.

She never expected to take him up on it.

She hadn't envisioned being a fugitive, either.

His letters had begun to worry her a couple of years later, just when she'd needed to put distance between herself and Vegas, where she'd finally landed in the chorus line. She'd been witness to a murder, but not an important enough one to merit witness protection. Still, the detective to whom she'd given her statement agreed that a disappearing act might be a great idea until crime boss Russ Bollinger was behind bars. In the process of figuring out where to relocate, she decided to pay Skeeter a visit and check on him.

Nearly a year later, she was still here and beginning to relax. After breaking a hip, Skeeter was in a nursing home until she could secure a place for him better than the ramshackle quarters he'd inhabited behind the bar. She, with not a shred of business experience, had scrambled to learn on the job, while running the enterprise that supported him.

To her surprise, she was managing to do just that.

She also had a goal, though how much she wanted it scared her to death.

Her objective was a house, but not just any house. Okay, just a cottage, but…The Perfect Cottage. One she would turn into her first real home.

If, that is, the owner would sell it.

"Last call, folks," Darrell said.

"Who's going to drive Bobby home?" she asked.

"I guess I could," Louie grumbled.

"Hell, no, you won't. You can't hardly see the road," Bobby complained.

"Larry, you drive him, and you—" she pointed at Bobby "—get up here and give me a dollar."

Over the grousing, she smiled. "Keep it up, gentlemen. Christmas is looking festive this year, and here we are, only March." A chorus of good-nights winged her way. More content than she'd ever imagined being, Jezebel set dirty glasses in the sink and began running water.

CHAPTER TWO

GROGGY FROM A RESTLESS NIGHT and three plane changes, Gamble trudged into the bright lights of the Dallas-Fort Worth terminal. He stopped to buy the biggest cup of coffee available, then made his way to baggage claim, where his brother would pick him up for the two-plus hour ride to Three Pines.

He burned his tongue on the hot drink and swore. Dropped his duffel and rubbed at the grit of travel. He couldn't spot Levi anywhere.

Then his sister, Lily, appeared before him. Grabbed him and held tight. "I could kill you," she whispered as she clung to his neck. "I missed you so much."

Gamble closed his eyes and hung on. For months after Charlotte's death, he'd locked himself in the cottage, refusing to speak to friends or family alike. He'd never meant to be cruel; it was simply that drawing the next breath felt beyond him most days.

But he realized now just how much he'd worried all of them. "I'm sorry."

Lily drew back. "You're here now. That's all that matters." She scrutinized him. "You're exhausted, I can see. But you're not such a ghost anymore, are you?"

His shoulders sagged. "No." Damn it all.

Lily plastered herself to his side, one arm around his waist. "You'd better not even think about leaving again."

He wouldn't begin with a promise he couldn't keep. He was here only to dispense with his past. "Where's Levi?"

"Behind you," said a male voice. "I can't decide whether to hug you or kick your ass."

"Take your pick. I wouldn't put up much of a battle." Gamble turned to face the year-older brother people said could be his twin. Levi's hair, however, was chestnut-brown, where Gamble's was black, and Levi's eyes were nearly navy, instead of Gamble's lighter blue.

"You look like hell," Levi said before pulling him into a fierce, back-slapping embrace.

After so long alone, Gamble had forgotten what it felt like to be with someone who loved him. He lingered longer than normal, and Levi didn't appear any more ready to let him go.

They broke apart, and Gamble saw a bright sheen in his brother's eyes that must have resembled that in his own.

Then he realized that Lily was openly crying, and Levi's cheer was forced.

"What's wrong?"

His siblings traded glances, then observed him as if measuring his resilience.

His chest constricted. "Is it Mom? What's happened?"

When they still hesitated, his temper stirred. "I'm not going to break. Tell me."

"She was in a wreck late last night."

"How bad?"

"A broken leg, a concussion, some internal bleeding. Car's totaled." Levi scrubbed at his face. "She made it through the surgery, but she's still unconscious. Noah's with her. The doctor says we shouldn't worry yet—"

"But you are."

Levi regarded Lily uneasily.

"You don't have to protect me, either," Lily said. "I'm not a kid, Levi. Yes, we're worried," she answered Gamble. "Mom has seemed...fragile lately."

"And no one told me?"

Levi's jaw tightened. "Would you have come?"

Gamble halted in midstep. "You're out of line."

"Guys," Lily cautioned. "Fighting won't help her."

Gamble continued as if she hadn't spoken. "You can't believe I wouldn't have been here in a heartbeat if I'd known." What if she never regained consciousness? How much time had he lost with her?

Levi raked fingers through his hair. "Of course you would. Mom and I actually had a fight over you."

"Me? Why?"

"The cottage. She didn't think I should make you return to deal with it."

"She believed I couldn't handle it." His jaw clenched. "I'm not a kid."

"She loves you, Gamble. She wants you to live again. She's ecstatic about the great reviews you've gotten for your show."

"She shouldn't be shielding me." It was hardly the first time, though. Marian Smith had never given up on her second son, even in the darkest days. It was she who had reminded Gamble of Charlotte's deep regret that he'd abandoned his art to care for her. She had let her son grieve longer than she'd wanted, but though she'd granted him room to find his way, she'd watched him with an eagle's eye. She'd slipped into the house and left him food each day when merely getting out of bed had been too much for him. Picked up the brushes he'd snapped like so many twigs during the rage that followed his one attempt to paint. Pressed a kiss to his hair when he'd sat on the porch, staring blindly.

Loved him far better and longer than he deserved.

And put him first, even when it hurt her for him to go.

"Let's hit the road."

"What's your bag look like? I'll get it."

"This is it."

"Gamble, you can't cut and run again, damn it."

"I didn't take much with me," Gamble explained.

"You've been gone a year and those're all the clothes you own?"

"Not everyone's a clotheshorse like Noah." Their younger brother had saved his allowance to buy an Izod shirt when he was seven.

Levi chuckled. "Lily would kill for half the wardrobe."

The three of them shared a faint smile, but their hearts weren't in it.

"I need to see her," Gamble said. "I'll never forgive myself if—"

Levi gave a sharp shake of the head. "Not gonna happen. Mom's tough."

"Not exactly the celebration we'd planned for her sixtieth birthday," Lily said, leaning into Gamble's side and suddenly sounding very young indeed.

He squeezed her shoulders as he and Levi shared a silent understanding. "Levi's right. Mom's a survivor. She'll be fine. We'll just postpone the party."

He kept his fears to himself. *Hold on, Mom. I'm so sorry. Please—*

But he wasn't certain with whom he was pleading, his mother or the God who had abandoned him on the day Charlotte died.

JEZEBEL STUBBED HER TOE on the ugliest couch in North America. She would have cursed, long and loudly, but she couldn't afford to break her own rule.

She sat on the couch she'd covered with a velveteen crazy quilt in vivid jewel tones and rubbed the offended toe.

"Mroww—" Oscar leaped from the stack of gardening books on the garage-sale coffee table to the sagging cushion beside her and tried to worm his way onto Jezebel's lap.

"The beer truck is coming. I don't have time for you," she complained. But she picked him up and rubbed her nose into his long black-and-white fur as her fingers went to work.

Soon, he was purring so loudly that Rufus ambled over from his spot by the space heater she liked to pretend was a fireplace. Ignoring the feline perched on one of her legs, he plopped his big, shaggy golden head on the other.

Jezebel chuckled as each refused to acknowledge the other's existence. The big old hound, part golden retriever and part heaven-knows-what, had been with her since she'd found him as a puppy, abandoned in the alley behind a strip joint in Tahoe. He was all she'd brought with her when she'd fled. She and Rufus had traveled many a mile together, and no cat, however fat or feisty, was going to ruffle him.

She indulged in a few moments of sheer sloth in a life that was seldom conducive, nuzzling and petting both animals until everyone was happy, herself included.

Pretty pathetic, Jez ol' girl. Admit it—you'd rather be wrapped around a good man.

Maybe so, but the sticking point was that word: *good.* She'd sworn off men and sex long before she'd left Vegas. Her life journey had put her in contact with too many males to count, but most of them were married and cheating or divorced and bitter…or just sorry in general.

She'd long ago made her peace with the tendency of redblooded males to ogle her generous proportions; she barely noticed it anymore. She and this figure had been cohabiting for a lot of years. It was a helpful tool, yes, but it was just as much a pain in her curvy behind.

She'd used it when she had to, but most times, she'd sell her soul for a pair of boyish hips and an A-cup bra. Okay, B. No need to get carried away.

Anyway, here in Three Pines, population seven hundred forty-nine, men like the one who'd fit her secret fantasy were simply a dream, as were the babies and white picket fence that were supposed to go with him. Oh, there was Levi Smith, the town's veterinarian and most eligible bachelor, but his type went for sweet and wholesome. Anyway, such fancies were absurd for a woman with her background, even if she'd ever tell anyone. Which she wouldn't.

But she had found the house part of the fantasy and drove by it at least once a week. It didn't belong to her yet, but she desperately wished for it to. Her carefully hoarded savings would make the down payment. She was determined that Skeeter would have a proper home in which to enjoy whatever days were left to him.

Jezebel Hart hadn't survived her rough-and-tumble life on good looks alone. She had grit aplenty, and she wasn't afraid of hard work. The cottage she already thought of as hers would require plenty of both. Like Sleeping Beauty, it had lain a long time beneath the tangled vines of heartache and loss, according to local lore.

She wanted to kiss it back to life.

She plucked the cat from her lap and gave Rufus one last rub, then rose. "Okay, guys, keep the party down. I'm off to work."

Then she went out the door of what barely qualified as a shanty, rounded the corner and entered the same building from the side, just as the beer truck rumbled into the parking lot.

GAMBLE PAUSED after leaving his mother's hospital room and scrubbed his hands over his face to dislodge the grip of despair. The too-familiar scents, antiseptics and cleansers, blood and sickness...and death.

On just such a night, he'd walked through these halls for the last time, rudderless and reeling. A *widower,* a term for someone who'd had a full life, who'd shepherded children to adulthood, seen silver strands weave themselves into his wife's hair and his own.

He had none of that—no wife, no child. Only a too-brief past that, despite all the worries over Charlotte's health, had sparkled with joy and love like diamond-bright drops of dew in a summer dawn.

And here he was again. The sight of his mother had been a fist to the heart. Even if he hadn't hated hospitals because he'd spent so many hours in them with Charlotte, he would have felt the impact of this. Marian Smith loved the outdoors; she should have sunshine on her face, not fluorescent lights. She ought to be surrounded by her flowers and herbs, not impersonal machines exuding beeps and heartless digital messages.

"Gamble?"

Reluctantly, he turned at the voice. Blinked. "Helen?"

Charlotte's best friend smiled. "How are you?"

"What are you doing here?"

She gestured to her scrubs. "I work here."

"I thought you lived in Dallas."

"My folks can't manage without help, so I'm back."

"What about Ricky?"

She shrugged. "We're divorced."

"I'm sorry."

"It happens."

A long, uncomfortable pause.

"Gamble, I never knew how to talk to you when Charlotte died."

He averted his eyes from the pity in hers. "There was nothing to say."

"I read about your show. Charlotte would be so proud."

"It's not—" *what I wanted. Not if losing her was the price.* But he kept silent.

"She loved you so much."

"Don't." The old fury whipped through him as if he'd never mastered it. He turned away, seeking an exit.

She grabbed his arm. "Gamble, she honestly believed she could bear that child for you and make your life together even better."

"Well, she didn't, did she?" Bile rose in his throat.

All the dark days rolled back over him like a menacing fog.

"You have to forgive her, Gamble. Put it behind you."

"Leave me alone," he all but shouted. With immense effort, he called back the beast that clamored to spread the hurt.

Palm out in warning, breath coming hard, he met her shocked gaze. "Helen, I'm sorry. I'm just not—"

Ready.

He fled past the crowded waiting room filled with his mother's friends and ducked into the stairwell. Halfway down a flight of steps, he sank onto the bottom one and tried to breathe. He couldn't deal with any more sympathy just now, or the pitying stares.

Or the knowledge that the progress he thought he'd made could be destroyed so easily.

After a few minutes, a door opened above him. "Gamble, you here?"

Gamble stirred. "Yeah. Come on down, Noah."

His younger brother descended and crouched beside him but didn't speak. Noah had always been the peacemaker. When Gamble and Levi were going at each other, over toys or chores or girls—or just for the fun of pounding a brother—Noah would step in and try to use logic.

He hadn't had a lot of success when the two of

them had their blood running high, but Gamble knew Levi felt as fiercely protective of their sibling as he did. "Sorry. I'll go back to wait with you all now."

"Doc told us to head out for the night. We can return in the morning, and he's got Levi's cell number to call at any time. Her vitals are good, and they think she's stable, that it's her body's protective reaction to stay under while she heals."

"I can't just leave her here like that."

Noah's gaze was sympathetic. "We all remember how you slept in chairs to be with Charlotte every minute. No one doubts your devotion, Gamble. But even if being inside a hospital wasn't making you crazy, there's nothing we can do right now but wait. Go home and get some rest. You look like something the cat dragged in."

He didn't attempt to deny how being in this place again impacted him. He sought a smile. "You're just jealous because I'm prettier."

Noah snickered and shoved him. "Believe me, bud, I'd be happier if you were." Noah's Newman-blue eyes and killer lashes, coupled with their mother's blond hair, were only some of the features that had made strangers stop their mother on the street to coo over him as a little boy. Now grown women did.

Though Noah had hated the reaction as a kid, he'd progressed to taking full advantage of it as a man.

"I'm serious, Gamble. Here are the keys to my car. I'll catch a ride with Levi. You staying at your house or Mom's?"

Gamble tensed. "I don't know." Either place held too many memories. "I guess I'll drive out to the cottage and check it out."

"You really going to sell it?"

Memory squeezed his heart in a merciless fist. "I haven't seen the offer."

Noah clapped one hand on his shoulder and stood. "All in good time. Get some sleep, bro. Everything will look different in the morning. Here's my cell, so we can phone you if Levi gets any word. Don't suppose a hermit has one."

"Nope." Gamble accepted the phone as if he'd been asked to pet a rattler. "How do you use it?"

Noah rolled his eyes. "One of these days, we're going to drag you into this century." Quickly, he demonstrated the rudiments.

Gamble rose and drew Noah into a bear hug. "Thanks." He clasped the keys and continued down the steps. He was exhausted but too wound up to sleep.

Might as well face the cottage.

As he exited the hospital, he noticed that the light was nearly gone. In the gathering shadows, he drove down tree-lined streets and out to the edge of town. He passed the closed-down Rialto movie theater and the old five-and-dime. A mile and a half down the main road, he turned at Ed's Feed and Grain, then after another mile, crossed the slow, syrupy ribbon the locals called Honey Creek.

Charlotte had loved its name. She'd requested a sign for their gate. Welcome To Honey Creek Cottage, it had proudly proclaimed. Her little haven in the woods.

Once his haven, too.

And someone now had the balls to try to buy it.

He hadn't even asked Levi how much was being offered. He should sell it, he knew. How could he ever live there again?

But how could he give away Charlotte's dream to a stranger? He stared at the landscape. The creek meandered along the southern boundary of the grand sum of seven acres he'd been able to afford. The red soil, more sand than clay, nurtured countless pines and shin oaks, sprinkled with native dogwoods here and there. Charlotte loved the fragile blossoms of the dogwood so much he'd planted them around the house, too, along with a couple of magnolias and too many azaleas to count. Both dogwoods and azaleas might be blooming already, he imagined.

And, of course, there were her roses, as lush and flamboyant as she was frail. If life had treated her better, she would have been just as vibrant.

But fate had given her no such chances, damn it all to hell.

As he neared the bend where the house would become visible, Gamble jammed on the brakes, a visceral dread snaking through him.

His breath came faster. He clutched the steering wheel with white-knuckled fingers and bowed his forehead against it.

For a long moment, the sound of his heartbeat was so loud nothing else could intrude. A train wailed in the distance, and he wanted to be on it. To dodge all the feelings roaring toward him, unleashed in spite of the ruthless control he'd exerted to avoid ever plunging into that dark place again.

A shred of self-preservation had him whipping the car around and racing in the opposite direction.

He couldn't face his mother's home yet, either, and he didn't want to talk to his siblings. There was one place that held no memories to drown him, an establishment he'd seldom entered, first because he was too young, then because he was already married to Charlotte and had no need to carouse.

Skeeter's Bar. He hardly ever drank. Had instinctively avoided it in the depths of mourning, unwilling to allow himself the escape of crawling into a bottle, never to emerge.

But tonight he had nowhere else he could bear to go.

JEZEBEL NOTICED the tall, rugged stranger the second he entered. There was something unsettling about the way he stalked across the floor and snagged a shadowed booth in the back. A restlessness akin to anger crackled in the air around him.

This was not a man who was comfortable inside his skin.

But he was sure good-looking.

Interest piqued, she moved to take his order.

"We don't know this guy, Jez. Be careful," Darrell said, his bartender's radar obviously picking up the same vibes.

"Always am," she replied as she passed him. Three Pines, Texas, had yet to throw anything at her to rock her confidence in her ability to handle the male of the species.

"What can I get you tonight?"

"A beer." The stranger never took his eyes off the scarred tabletop. "And a shot," he added.

"Tap or bottle?"

"Either." One finger tapped a staccato on the surface.

"Jack Black?"

"Whatever."

"Anything to eat with that?"

"Nope."

She paused, then thought better of the urge to ask what was wrong. Most drinkers cared about the selection. He was either caught in a craving or had little experience. Either way, he'd warrant watching. "Coming up."

When she returned, she laid down a coaster and set the mug atop it with the shot glass beside it.

"Fancy for Skeeter's," he observed. Then, as if he regretted the impulse, he clamped his mouth shut.

"I made a few changes."

"Why?" His gaze slid upward.

"Skeeter asked me to run the place." She prepared herself for the usual leer.

Instead, he stared right through her. "Where is he?"

"Is he a friend?"

"No. I didn't come around here." The impassive gaze darkened.

"Why not?"

He didn't answer, but his grip tightened on the mug.

"Sorry. Occupational hazard. You get used to people telling you their stories."

"I'll spare you mine." A brush-off if ever she'd heard one.

Hardly the usual masculine reaction to her. Not that she was complaining. "Your call." She shrugged. "Want me to start you a tab?"

He was silent so long she wondered if she should repeat the question.

Then he peered up at her, eyes sharp with pain before they quickly shuttered. "Yeah."

She nearly offered to sit down and listen to whatever was wrong, but just then, she heard the unmistakable sounds of an argument beginning at the pool table.

"I'll check back." Preferring to handle the fracas herself before Darrell had to crack heads, she made her way toward the source of the trouble.

SKEETER HAD HIM a looker in charge, didn't he? Gamble watched the bombshell's progress across the bar. Not his type, but there was no question she could make a man drool. He'd bet she neared six feet in those boots, and the body beneath the curve-hugging jeans and tight red tank was lush and ripe. Sexgoddess hot, even before you took in the black curls tumbling down her back. And her legs were endless.

Then there was that voice—wet-dream, phonesex husky. What the hell was someone like that doing in Three Pines, running Skeeter's bar?

He picked up the shot and drained it, then chased it with the beer.

And scowled. Neither beverage was likely to ease the itch under his skin that had him wanting to get back in Noah's jazzy car and drive as far and fast as he could to escape what being in this town did to him.

"Aw, Jezebel, goddammit, he started it," one man complained.

"That's four dollars, Chappy. Want to go for eight?"

Jezebel. Of course that would be her name. He had no difficulty seeing men dropping left and right at her feet, felled by a siren.

But at the moment, the two who'd been ready to cross pool cues and charge into battle had their heads hanging like scolded pups.

Gamble frowned and followed the direction she was pointing. The bartender shoved a jar across the bar, and Chappy Martinez, who'd worked at the butane dealership since Gamble was a kid, scuffed his way toward it, then stuffed the bills inside.

"You, too, Joe Mack," she continued. "I heard what you said. Your first offense of the night, and I'd just love for you to go for two." No queen was ever more imperious.

Gamble speculated on what might be written on the jar's label. Maybe he'd ask the next time she came over.

A fast scan around showed that the place had changed in other ways. The floor no longer was caked with grime, and the cheap paneling had been painted. Much was left as he remembered it, but the general air of seediness had been dispelled.

Then his jaw dropped. Oh, man. There was a fern hanging in the corner. Skeeter must surely be dead.

If not, the old reprobate would be, once he learned that she was making a fern bar out of the most disreputable joint in three counties.

He drained his beer and realized he was a little dizzy. He'd better eat after all. Before he could summon her, though, she materialized with a refill in her hands, balanced alongside a set of onion rings. "You said you weren't hungry, but it's starting to rain, and I'm not sending anyone home drunk. You should put something in your stomach."

"Is this a bar or a day care? And where the hell is Skeeter? Besides, how do you know I haven't already eaten?"

One eyebrow lifted, and she sighed. "You're new, so I'll give you a pass this one time."

"For what?"

She nodded toward the jar. "No profanity. First offense, you pay a dollar. Doubles each time after that. Each night you get a reset to zero. I believe in rehabilitation."

Stunned to speechlessness, he reared back and stared at her.

She lifted one shoulder. The big gold hoops at her ears bobbed. "Those're the rules."

A rusty chuckle erupted, surprising them both. "You're kidding."

"Nope."

"Or what?"

"You have to leave. Pay up or get out."

"That's highway robbery."

Pure mischief glittered in eyes that were as emerald a green as he'd ever seen. "My place, my rules."

"Skeeter must be rolling over in his grave."

"He's not dead." But sorrow shifted in her expression.

"Where are you hiding him, and is he aware that you're ruining his bar?"

"He trusts my judgment."

"But you've—" Gamble gestured around the room. "Cleaned up. Hung a damn fern," he spluttered.

"The place needs it." She proffered a palm. "That'll be a dollar."

"I'll run a tab." He crossed his arms over his chest.

"Sorry—jar doesn't extend credit."

"Bet you don't get much in the way of tips with an attitude like that."

She drew in a breath with that magnificent chest and placed one hand on a hip his fingers had an urge to sample. "You'd be wrong." Her eyes sparkled with amusement.

Another laugh rumbled out of his throat. When was the last time he'd felt like laughing? He reached for his wallet, extracted a bill and prepared to rise.

She plucked it from his hand. "I'll do it for you

on my way to order your hamburger. Medium rare, I'm guessing."

"I'm not—" He glanced at the plate he didn't recall emptying. *Hungry.* "You are one scary woman."

"You betcha. Medium-rare hamburger, Darrell," she hollered as she sauntered back across the room.

Gamble's mouth watered, and he wasn't at all sure the food was responsible.

JEZEBEL SMILED to herself as she bantered with the regulars.

Misery had dug claws into that man before he'd ever walked in the door, yet she had managed to make him laugh.

Sexy and sad…was there ever a more potent combination?

And if that's not a fool's game, Jezebel, I can't imagine what is. He's got a heartbreaker's eyes and a sinner's mouth. You are just looking for trouble.

Probably so, but she could keep it to a harmless flirtation. Fun for her, and much needed, she sensed, for him.

Wouldn't do to let herself get out of practice, now would it? And when again was such eye candy likely to walk through her door?

"Food's ready," Darrell called out from the kitchen.

She went after it.

"I'll take it to him," Darrell offered.

"Darrell, I don't need a keeper."

"You might." He scowled in the stranger's direction.

"He's just lonely."

"And you aren't?"

Her eyes widened. "Of course not."

"I don't pry, Jez, but you been here nearly a year and still no one knows much about you, where you come from or such. Not anybody's business, but it hasn't escaped me that I never see you with a soul outside this bar."

"I visit Skeeter."

"Don't be dense."

"Men aren't part of the picture for now. Not that I should have to explain."

"Goes without saying. Tell me anyway."

"This burger will get cold."

He stopped her with a hand on her arm. "Chappy recognizes him, I think, and Louie, too. I'm going to check him out."

She shook her head, absurdly warmed. "Darrell, I have no use for a daddy. I'm not running away with the man—I'm just serving him supper."

"And I'll be watching him, every step." His jaw set. Darrell was easygoing for the most part, but he could be extremely stubborn when provoked.

She smiled. "You're a good friend. Thanks for

worrying over me." She turned to leave. "You ask me, though, I believe someone in this kitchen could use an uninterrupted night's sleep. Why don't you take off early. I can handle the cleanup by myself."

"Maybe. If that man ain't still hangin' around."

"Sugar, if he's not, I've lost my touch."

CHAPTER THREE

FOR TWO HOURS NOW, Gamble had barely budged from the booth, as he settled back on the cushions while letting his mind slip into neutral between visits from the puzzling Jezebel. When things slowed now and again, she sat with him and entertained him with stories about the locals, interspersed with some of the most deft flirting he'd ever experienced.

Her zest for life had relentlessly brushed away his gloom, sweeping it out the door and leaving a surprising lightness behind. He'd kept to himself in Manhattan, maintaining a ruthless grip on the emotions that had nearly destroyed him after Charlotte died; he didn't kid himself that he was fit company for anyone. He was holding himself together by sheer will, stumbling his way without grace into living again while wondering, most of the time, why he bothered. Only understanding what losing him would do to his family had made him try, and he'd had to get out of Three Pines to stand a chance.

Painting was his lone outlet, the sole occasion on which he allowed color into his bare-bones existence, but even then, it was almost as though he watched a stranger, possessed by the scouring whip of tenderness lost and hungers turned feral, create them.

The only emotions he felt anymore were the dark ones. This visit from the alien lighter side baffled him.

As did the increasing appetite no hamburger could satisfy. Her tongue had a way of slicking over one corner of her upper lip that drained all the blood from his head. She wasn't even aware she was doing it, he didn't think.

Or was she? With a mouth designed for seduction as much as the rest of her flagrant curves, how could she not be?

But he was grateful, whatever her intent, for the way she'd yanked his mind right out of his troubles.

He'd talked to Levi, who'd promised again to call him, should anything change. Just to be sure, though, he'd phoned the hospital himself. His mother's vitals still looked positive, and they'd upgraded her condition. He'd been advised to get a good night's sleep—but that was the problem.

He had no desire to go either to the cottage or to his mother's house. He could bunk at Levi's, but his brother the vet had a stacked schedule of appointments;

Gamble didn't want to risk waking him. And Three Pines didn't possess even a kissing cousin to a motel.

So Gamble stayed in his booth as the crowd thinned.

Chappy, one of the stragglers still present, stopped by. "Heard about your mama. How's she doing?"

"She's holding her own."

"She's a great lady."

"You won't get any argument from me."

Chappy shifted on his feet as if he was tempted to say more, but finally he simply nodded. "Well, better to be getting on home. Nice to see you, Gamble."

"You, too, Chappy." Gamble nearly followed as the restlessness seized him again. He'd grown accustomed to the anonymity of Manhattan and the constant activity available to serve as distraction. He wasn't ready to deal with all the memories, both his and others', that lay waiting around every corner.

Gone crazy, would have been the town's verdict. *Man done lost his mind.*

If so, they weren't wrong. He still felt half-insane at times. The ache might have lost some of its bite, but it was far from vanquished, as the contretemps with Helen had made clear.

No reason he should have ease. Charlotte was the one love of his life, and she'd died thinking he was still angry. A man didn't deserve to find peace after that.

Gamble glanced around and realized that nearly

everyone was gone. The burly bartender had one very inebriated customer in hand and was escorting him out to the parking lot. Jezebel toted a full tray of empties toward the bar.

Just then, a man arrayed in excessive leather and chains emerged from the hall leading to the bathrooms and made a beeline for her. Intent on her burden, she didn't spot the guy until he'd crowded her against the bar.

Gamble couldn't hear what they were saying, but he didn't like the man's body language or the fact that he outweighed Jezebel by a good fifty pounds, even if much of it was beer belly.

He rose just as the man's beefy arm snaked around Jezebel's waist. Saw her shy away, but she had nowhere to retreat.

"Hey—" he called out.

The guy's head whipped around, and small, mean eyes glared at him. "Beat it."

Gamble neared, grabbed the guy's shoulder and shoved him back, placing his own body between the man and Jezebel. "Make me." Something a little nasty and mean inside him itched for the creep to rise to the challenge.

The stench of alcohol rose from his opponent's pores, blasted from his breath. "The bimbo ain't yours. What the hell do you care?" With more quickness than Gamble would have credited him, he sneaked out a punch at Gamble's head.

Gamble's own reflexes were slowed by the drinks he'd consumed. The blow glanced off his skull before he could dodge it, but he managed to land one in the guy's doughy gut. The man staggered, and Gamble caught him with a punch square on the chin.

He went down like a felled log.

Gamble stood over him. Straightened. "She's not a bimbo," he said to the stunned, blinking man.

The loaded tray crashed to the bar and glasses rattled.

Gamble whirled to catch her—

Only to see Jezebel regarding him quizzically. "I could have dealt with him, you know. He's not the first drunk who's ever accosted me."

He frowned. "You had your hands full. Like me to apologize?"

Her expression cleared. "No," she said quietly. "I want to say thank you. It's…nice. I've been fending for myself for a long time." She stepped closer, examining him. "How's the head?"

"Better than his." And Gamble found himself grinning.

She grinned back.

The guy at his feet groaned.

"I'll get him out of here," Gamble offered, and bent to the task of hauling the man up.

"What's going on?" the returning bartender asked.

"This gentleman came to my rescue, Darrell." Her tone held an odd note, as if the two of them were communicating on another level.

"Sorry, Jez."

"You were a little occupied."

"I thought Manny was the last one."

"This fellow was in the bathroom," Gamble said.

"Well." The giant shrugged. "I'll send him on his way." Then, as if the burly drunk were a feather-weight, Darrell hefted him over his shoulder and carted him out.

Gamble watched him go with some amazement. "Wow."

Jezebel chuckled. "Yeah. Darrell's a phenomenon."

But soon, the climate in the room shifted. Gamble looked at her.

She looked right back at him.

The temperature bumped up a notch.

Finally, she broke the humming silence. "Uh, how about some ice for your head?"

He thought it was the scent of her more than the blow that had his head spinning. "I'm okay."

Still neither moved.

Gamble was aware that he should go.

But he didn't want to. "Could you use some help?" His glance encompassed the room. "You've had a long night."

He recognized the answering temptation in her. Practically feel the current zipping between them. "No longer than usual."

He wasn't sure what would happen if he pressed to stay. Wasn't positive what he wished would happen.

Darrell walked in, and Gamble and Jezebel jumped apart guiltily.

Jezebel hastily began placing chairs on top of tables, moving away from him. Darrell followed her and joined in, arguing with her in low tones.

At last, the giant stalked over to him with fire in his eyes.

"Not that I'm not grateful to you for layin' that jerk out. Jezebel can't always control ever'thin' she believes she can." He leaned into Gamble. "Irregardless, if you harm one hair on her head, I will hunt you down like a dog."

Gamble did a double take, then noticed Jezebel shaking her head.

"Darrell, if you don't beat it this minute, you're fired."

The man snorted. "You didn't hire me and you can't fire me."

"Then I'm telling Shirley on you."

The fierce eyes rolled. A smile twitched his lips. "I can handle my wife."

"Like me to ask her opinion on that?"

"I'm going, I'm going." He paused and leaned closer to Gamble. "Chappy and Louie vouch for you, or I'd stay here, no matter what she says."

"I don't know what you think I'm going to do, but I get the message."

"Good." He nodded and left.

Gamble remained standing. With the room emptied of the clamor of so many personalities, the undertow between the two of them intensified.

"Just ignore him," she remarked as she began to mop. "He has this idea I'm some sort of fragile flower."

So matter-of-fact, as if the atmosphere weren't humming.

Gamble attempted to match her tone. "Compared with him, anyone is." Making a decision, he walked to her and held out his hand. "I can manage this while you do something more challenging."

She paused. "If I have an urge to jump your bones, I don't require you to earn it."

"That's blunt."

"No reason to pretend we're not attracted. You need romancing, sugar?"

"Got some sass on you, don't you?"

One eyebrow lifted. "I do, at that. Wanna make

something of it?" She slid one scarlet-tipped nail down the center of his chest.

The hum built to a roar. What the hell. They were both adults. He grabbed the mop with one hand and hooked the other around her neck. Leaned in and brushed his lips over hers to test them both.

A faint, breathy moan purred from her throat.

Then she slicked her tongue over his mouth.

Opened her eyes and stared at him while sliding her tongue over her lips, tasting him. "Yum."

Every other thought in his head vanished. He bent to the task of kissing her socks off.

She responded in kind, and for endless seconds, they were locked in an unashamedly carnal embrace.

Then she slapped one hand on his chest and stepped back. "You mop and I'll finish over there."

Her glide away from him was pure sex kitten. Gamble welcomed the surge of heat, grateful for the respite. With any luck, they'd both feel better in an hour.

Then he watched the sway of those hips.

Okay, two hours. Minimum.

He began mopping…and found himself smiling.

JEZEBEL WAS JUST ABOUT to lose her nerve, when the jukebox started. She talked a good game, but it had been a long time for her, and she'd nurtured the idea that when she next had sex, it would be with someone who mattered.

But he'd leaped to her rescue. She considered the misery and loneliness she'd read in his eyes, felt the echo of her own. Whoever he was, the denizens of the bar approved of him. No matter how raucous the byplay between them and her, they were very protective of her. She hadn't asked anyone for his story, but it was clear from their reactions that though most of them gave him wide berth, it had to do with consideration, not fear.

And though she'd made a lot of mistakes in her life, she had excellent radar for human nature.

His hand on her shoulder jolted her. "Dance with me," he said.

She blinked. "Dance?"

"Yeah. You know, two people stand close, move around the floor?"

Despite his casual tone, she saw nerves in him, too, and the knowledge warmed her. "You got a name?"

He seemed surprised. "No one told you?"

"I didn't inquire. People deserve privacy."

"Tell that to a small town."

"A lesson I'm learning. My name's Jezebel Hart." She held out a hand, though a handshake seemed awkward. But where were the rule books for an occasion like this?

He clasped hers in his own and somehow made her feel delicate, not a reaction she was used to. "Gamble Smith."

They stood there for a moment as self-conscious as any she could recall.

Then it hit her. Gamble Smith. The man who'd built the house she treasured. For the wife he'd lost, along with their unborn child.

Oh, lordy. No wonder she'd picked up on his sorrow. The story was a local legend—how he'd locked himself in that place for months, then finally left town.

Obviously, he still wasn't over the tragedy.

And this was definitely not the time to bring up her intention to buy his cottage.

Besides, his mother, Marian, was in the hospital, she'd heard earlier tonight. Lots of women in the town had given Jezebel a cold shoulder, but his mother wasn't one of them. Their paths hadn't crossed much; when they had, though, Marian had been nothing but polite and helpful, even warm.

He must be half out of his mind with worry, and she could tell that he was on the verge of running out the door, no matter how lonely he was, or how haunted.

He needed the respite. She could give it to him.

She seized the initiative. "Pleased to meet you, Gamble Smith. So are we going to dance or what?"

He studied her with suspicion, as though on alert for pity.

She made certain he found none, only challenge.

Finally, he exhaled in a gust. "Yeah. We're going to dance." But his shoulders stiffened as he took her in his arms, keeping a careful distance between them.

This man was hurt, all right, and it went deep. He held her as if he hadn't done this in a very long time.

Jezebel was more accustomed to fending off advances, not putting forth her own, but innate compassion had her longing to reach out. She bridged some of the gap between them, then lightly turned her forehead into his strong throat, coming as near to a hug as he'd likely let her.

He tensed at first, but when she didn't move again, he eased a little. She had a sense of time holding its breath to see what would happen.

Meanwhile, her own body couldn't seem to help reacting to his. He was all man, tall and powerfully built, if gaunt. Big enough to handle her, which was a novel experience. She towered over most males and had long ago learned to use that in her favor.

She wasn't sure what to think of Gamble Smith. Restless and angry one minute; heartbreakingly sad beneath. Lonely when she was sure he didn't have to be, not when he could kiss like that. She had a sense of being given a lit stick of dynamite. She had no wish to worsen things for him, but she wasn't sure how to avoid it.

"You ever relax? I can practically hear your brain clicking."

Her head rose in surprise. "I relax."

"How many hours have you been on your feet today?"

Her forehead wrinkled. "Why do you care?"

"It occurs to me that you might prefer to get off them."

He was worrying over her. She had to step carefully or she'd start to imagine more than this was.

She cast a cocky smile. "Is that a come-on?"

He blinked. "Would it work?"

She told the truth whenever possible. "Given the way you kiss, it just might. You up for a hard night of sweaty sex, cowboy?"

She'd expected a quick acceptance, but he surprised her. "I don't know." He stared off over her shoulder.

She snagged him back. "Let's check." She plastered herself against the front of him and stood on her toes to kiss him.

After an initial hesitation, he took charge.

And Jezebel's head swam.

SWEET MERCY, was all Gamble could think. He had an armful of woman, ripe and willing, and most of his brainpower had evaporated like mist in morning sun.

But he couldn't, in conscience, chance a repeat of what had happened with Kat. He broke off the kiss and held Jezebel at arm's length. "Only sex, right?"

"Huh?" Her eyes cleared gradually. He caught a flash that might have been hurt, but if so, she traded it instantly for a smile. "Of course. Just scratching an itch."

"You sure?"

She tilted her chin. "You used to women falling in love with you on sight, is that it?"

He had to chuckle. "Not hardly."

"I've never understood why men assume they're the only ones who can appreciate the value of a good tango in the sheets without getting their hearts all torn up. I'm no delicate violet, Gamble."

Charlotte had been, but this woman could not be more different. Determined not to think about Charlotte any more tonight, he gave Jezebel's knockout figure a slow scan. "A tropical hibiscus is more like it, all scarlet and showy and stop-your-heart gorgeous."

"So are we through examining our navels?" Her grin was pure mischief.

And contagious. With an easier heart than he'd had in days, Gamble smiled. "Yeah, I believe we are. Let's try this again."

He brought her close and tortured himself by cruising his mouth just above her skin. She smelled like glory. Felt like heaven, all those abundant curves, that temptress hair. "I have to paint you," he muttered. He could already visualize her, a siren in vivid carmine and gold, cobalt blue and the exact green of those stunning eyes.

She slid her hands into his hair and tugged. "Talk later. Kiss now." With strength garnered from carrying heavy trays of glasses, she pitted her impulse against his control. "It's been a long time for me." She stood on her tiptoes and snapped the bonds of his self-discipline.

Half-blind with craving, he grasped her hips and lifted her. "Wrap those long legs around me, damn it."

"I'm too heavy."

"Nuh-uh." He quieted her protest with his mouth, hitched her up and walked them to the nearest booth, every step rubbing his groin against hers and ratcheting the heat between them higher. He settled her on the table's edge, reluctant to lose the friction. He grasped for what fleeting control he could muster, painstakingly unbuttoned her blouse and nuzzled each new patch of flesh revealed.

Jezebel moaned and sank back on her elbows, the long line of her throat displayed as her hair tumbled behind her in glorious profusion.

Gamble paused to simply enjoy the sight. "You take my breath away."

Heavy-lidded, she smiled and arched her back. "Come here, and I'll take your virtue next."

He gave a hoarse shout of laughter. Fun had been in short supply for a long time. He savored it.

He pushed one hand into his pocket and hoped to heaven he'd replaced the condom in his wallet. When he found it, he brandished it as if it were diamonds.

Jezebel looked disappointed. "Only one?"

"We'd better make it count, huh?"

"Oh, we will, I promise you that." She cast him an impish grin. "But I have more if you're up for it."

His jeans were so uncomfortable he would surely die, and he couldn't help feeling grateful to her for keeping this simple and natural. Playful.

He cocked one eyebrow as he divested her of her boots. "I don't believe you should worry on that score—" Her jeans followed, and he sucked in a breath. "Where's the fine jar?"

"What?"

"Sweet hell, Jezebel—" He stopped and simply stared. The plain white cotton underwear couldn't disguise the bounty before him.

He was more than surprised when she crossed her arms over her chest and sat up.

"What's wrong?" he asked.

It was her turn to stare into the distance. She closed her eyes and bit her lip. "Nothing."

"Talk to me. What did I do?" When she remained silent and reached for her shirt, he cast about in his mind for the culprit.

And the significance of the simple cotton underwear hit him. With a name and figure like hers, she probably had guys slobbering over her all the time. Just because she had the appearance of a sex goddess didn't mean she felt like that inside.

He brushed her hands away and began buttoning her shirt himself. "I'm sorry. I guess men always swallow their tongues around you, don't they?"

A flick of surprise. "Most of them have no idea what my face looks like. They never get past my chest."

He lifted her chin. "Your face is as gorgeous as the rest of you, but I suspect there's more inside, isn't there?"

Wary eyes greeted his. "What gives you that idea?"

"Tell me about the No Profanity jar. What do you do with the proceeds?"

She shrugged. "Nothing special." She bent to grab her jeans.

He stayed her hands before she could don them. "That's not my bet. And why is it that you have the rule anyway? People come to bars to drink and raise hell."

She tossed that magnificent mane and jutted her chin. "No, they don't. They come for family."

He goggled, but it dawned on him that she was dead on the mark. "I'll be damned."

"That's eight dollars you owe me now."

"No," he said quietly. "I also owe you an apology."

She stilled. Exhaled. "You make it tough to be upset with you."

"Not if you get to know me. There are women in New York happy to confirm that." He paused. "Would you rather I go?"

She studied him for long seconds.

"No big deal." He turned away.

"Gamble."

He halted, still facing the door.

"Sometimes just getting through the night is important."

He stiffened. "I don't need your pity."

"I wasn't referring to you. Or not only you."

He heard her approach, and he still didn't move. She wrapped her arms around his waist from the back, and he attempted to ignore the feel of her, but it wasn't working.

"You're free to leave, but I won't make you regret it if you stay. I know about your wife, and I'm not out to take her place. No one could."

He swallowed hard and shut his eyes against the kindness in her voice.

"Go on, then," she said. Cool air slid between them as she retreated. "I won't beg."

He relented. Saw need in her, too, beyond the physical. "Come here." But he bridged the gap first. "You're right, but consider yourself forewarned. I won't be here long, and I'll never let my heart get involved with a woman again. If you can accept those conditions, then tonight nothing exists but you and me. No past, no future. Deal?"

He waited, sure she'd throw him out. His proposal was, after all, a damn cold-hearted way to go into what could only be physical release. He'd be attentive and give her what he had to offer, but it wasn't much.

Suddenly, he was exhausted; weary in soul more than body. This woman probably deserved better, and in another existence, maybe he would, too. But he'd had the kind of love you only get once in a lifetime, if you're very lucky, and he'd squandered it.

He looked away from the green eyes that studied him so intently. "Never mind. I wouldn't agree, either, if I were you."

She detained him with one hand on his elbow. Slowly, she softened against him. One hand slipped into his hair as she drew his head down toward her.

The love-goddess body brushed over the front of him, and heat rose again between them.

And that husky bedroom voice answered at last. "Deal."

CHAPTER FOUR

SHE KEPT HIM CLOSE to her as they left through the side door. Gamble was glad for the contact, because once she'd brought up Charlotte, he was about two steps away from running. His body was absolutely sure of what it wanted; his mind, still more logical than he'd like, was barely half-convinced. His heart? That cursed organ persisted in surviving, no matter how often he'd tried to starve it out of existence, and it was miserable. Torn between the battering of guilt and a yearning to escape the loneliness that was his self-imposed prison. Afraid that finding even a moment's surcease was so wrong that the punishment would be levied in some cosmic toll—perhaps his mother's health.

All the way around the building, his pace dragged. "Where are we going?"

Jezebel dropped his hand. "I'm headed in there," she said, indicating a door on the back side of the bar. "But you're leaving. You don't want to be here, and I'm not that hard up."

In the light from the parking lot, he could see her cheeks stained with color. Shame rose. "No." His voice was hardly audible. He cleared his throat and tried again. "I do want to be with you, Jezebel. If you'll have me."

She remained still, placing on him the burden of convincing her.

And his fears that this would be another Kat situation eased. This woman had more control of her emotions. With Kat, sex had been all thunder and fury and drama to hide a terrifying vulnerability. A heart that demanded an answering opening of the self from him...something he would never again share. All that was tender in him had died with Charlotte.

Jezebel's looks might be flamboyantly sexy, but he had a sense of a stalwart inner gate that guarded the woman inside. She might share her body, but she would not easily expose her core.

Which was a relief. Jezebel could protect herself, he felt certain. Lonely she might be, but not needy, and therefore, not a threat.

She wouldn't have to be alone tonight, and neither would he. Gamble locked away any misgivings and let body speak to body, the only language in which he was fluent with women.

Taking a chance, he slicked his tongue down her neck and taunted the delicate slope of her collarbone.

She inhaled sharply. Dug her fingers into her jeans. Gamble smiled and began to work his way into the teasing hollow of her cleavage, gently separating the panels of her shirt once more.

Her hands rose from her sides, then fluttered helplessly downward again. She murmured something in that unbelievably erotic voice, and Gamble's body reacted.

"Keys," she said, as her back arched. "Dropped them."

He caught a glint of metal. Anchoring one hand on her hip to prolong the contact, he bent and retrieved them. "Which one?"

Her unfocused gaze aroused him unmercifully. He scrambled to follow the pointed finger and jabbed that key in the lock before returning his attention to her brain-draining mouth.

Jezebel moaned and gripped his hands, placing them squarely on her very abundant breasts.

Her very *natural* breasts, he registered in the millisecond before he quit thinking at all.

After that came a ballet of farcical proportions as they did their best to get inside and move across the floor without relinquishing one micron of contact with the other's body. Gamble saw nothing of his surroundings, had only the vague impression of a hissing cat and a scrambling dog. He carted Jezebel across a blessedly small space toward the bed she indicated between devouring kisses, her legs locked around his hips, his hands filled with hers.

He managed to kick the door shut before he fell onto the bed with her, and they proceeded to thoroughly lose their minds.

Sighs and moans and whispers…fingers trailing over curves, hands grasping hardness. The glide of his tongue over her sweet inner hollows…her raven curls sliding across his belly.

"Gamble, now. Please, now. I can't—"

Instead, he drew her along on another wild ride into bliss.

At last, she unbalanced him, pinned him to the mattress and straddled him, condom brandished with a smile gleaming triumph. Nipples erect, skin blooming rose, hair a-tumble, she poised above him and began to apply the protection with her mouth.

Gamble bucked teasingly to unseat her, and reveled in the novelty of this woman who made him remember how to play. With Charlotte, everything had been so serious—

No. Not Charlotte. Don't think about—

But he couldn't help reacting.

Jezebel noticed, and froze. Withdrew.

Fury at himself took over then. Ruthlessly, he flipped her and entered her in one thrust, then set a hard pace. Charlotte was dead and he was alive, however often he'd wished different. His mother was hurt and his life was a sham and—

Jezebel was crying.

He flinched. Pulled away.

"No." She stared at him with so many expressions skating over her face that he couldn't interpret. Fierce determination. Hunger. Sorrow and, damn her, pity.

"Don't you feel sorry for me. Don't you dare," he growled.

Her expression was stricken. "It's not—"

He kissed her to shut her up. All playfulness vanished, and the two joined battle, only Gamble couldn't figure out if he was fighting her or himself.

Jezebel's back arched, those long, muscular legs locked him to her, and his twice-damned body betrayed him.

When his brain cleared, his head lay on her bosom as her hand stroked over his hair. For once, his mind was quiet and still. For a breathless, forbidden moment, he allowed himself to simply be.

How long since he'd known even a moment's peace? One stray beam of sunshine and hope. Of…connection.

It felt so good. Too good.

He couldn't see her expression without moving, and he wasn't sure he was brave enough to chance it, anyway. He didn't know whether to apologize or say thank you, to run like hell or stay and make it up to her.

Before he could figure it out, her body began to slacken into slumber. When her breathing settled into a slow, easy rhythm, he peeled himself from her.

And saw tears dried into silver tracks over skin like white velvet.

But her mouth was curved in a smile.

Gamble lay back for a minute and tried to decide if he was the most pathetic loser or sorriest bastard he'd ever known.

Ah, Charlotte. What did you ever find to love in me? He spoke, as he often did, to the woman whose memory proved elusive when he needed it most. He couldn't remember how her voice sounded anymore, and he was losing his hold on too much else.

He had to summon the strength to paint her portrait before he lost her altogether.

Gamble removed himself from Jezebel's bed as quietly as possible. On silent feet, he gathered his clothes and left without looking back.

Those extra condoms wouldn't be required tonight.

JEZEBEL AWOKE when the door clicked shut.

Heavenly days. Delicious echoes of his lovemaking still shivered through her body. Gamble Smith was a complicated mixture of raw physical power and staggering finesse. Hard, ropy muscles, long, virtuoso fingers and a sixth sense for a woman's sweet spots.

All of that mingled with enough shadows and pain to break your heart.

She sighed and rolled over, gathering his pillow to her as she had wanted to cuddle him. Shield him. *Boy, you sure can pick 'em, can't you?*

But Gamble Smith wasn't a child she could nurture or a stray like Rufus or Oscar that she could simply sweep up and incorporate into her life. She had her hands full, in any case, with Skeeter and the bar.

And Gamble didn't want to be tended; he'd made that perfectly clear.

Even if his body had responded differently at the end there. She didn't think he was aware of how tightly he'd clung to her, but he'd raised a riot of feelings. Her body still tingling from his, her heart twisting in sorrow, she'd also felt the bite of shame that he thought her so pathetic that he'd grant her mercy sex.

She shoved the pillow to the floor; Oscar yowled and scampered away. Instantly, Jezebel rolled and held out her hand. "I'm sorry. Come here," she entreated. With the slow disdain only a cat can muster, Oscar avoided her.

"You and Gamble have a lot in common." Just then, Rufus nudged her hip with his cold, wet nose.

She turned to him in gratitude. "And you're too much like me, aren't you, boy? Always hungry for affection." She sighed and shook her head. "Well, that man is a fool's errand, no matter how much he needs love."

No one had ever stuck by her in all her life; still, she'd never been able, in a small, secret part of her, to quit wishing for that special someone. Even to flirt with the notion now was emotional suicide, however, particularly given what she understood of Gamble and his past.

She glanced at the cat, a cool distance apart, occupied in grooming himself, so sure of his place in the world and caring not a fig for anyone else's desires.

She pressed a kiss to Rufus's head. "We could both learn a lesson from the Emperor here."

Rufus swiped his tongue over her cheek and nudged closer.

Jezebel chuckled and cast the night away like broom-swept dust. "I know, I know. We're both too old to change, aren't we? Good thing that man is leaving town soon. We'll just hope he doesn't come back into the bar before he goes."

Then she sobered. How would he feel about her offer to buy his cottage now?

Borrowing trouble, Jez. Nothing you can do about it tonight. With a shake of her head, she rose.

And felt an unmistakable wetness trailing down her thighs—

Left by a broken condom.

CHAPTER FIVE

OH, NO. No. What if I'm—

Jezebel sank onto one of her two mismatched kitchen chairs and tried to pinch off the word, but it wouldn't be forestalled.

Pregnant. She couldn't be, that was all. The odds were high against it, and she should be relieved. She had no business with a baby, not without a husband, however much she longed for a child. Single parenthood might be fine for some people, but not for someone with her background. What did she know about mothering? She'd been left on her own for days at a time until the child welfare people finally removed her from the junkie aunt who'd taken her in to collect child-welfare payments, and no one after that had wanted her.

But a *baby*... Regardless of the lousy timing, she couldn't help going gooey inside at the thought.

Jezebel cherished the few remnants of memory of her brief life with a whole family. She had been surrounded by love once, and she wished that for any child she might bear. One parent could give it, sure, but the small Jezebel had treasured her mother's gentleness and her father's strength; both had contributed to the sense of haven a little girl had assumed was normal.

However badly she craved to be a mother someday, she desired just as much for any child of hers to have that wealth. The loss was forever an ache inside her.

"Good grief." She shoved out of her chair. "It only happened a few hours ago, and I'm acting as if a baby is a done deal." She busied herself making coffee and starting breakfast.

Gamble Smith would have to be some kind of stud to knock her up the first time they'd made love—

Had sex, she corrected herself.

But she could still feel his hair beneath her fingers, thick and sable-dark, as he laid his head over her heart for those few moments when he'd let down the mile-high walls.

That poor man. He didn't appreciate her pity, and he was anything but weak, yet she couldn't help wishing to heal him.

Rufus ambled up and leaned against her leg in that funny way of his, as though he must be propped up. She cooed to him as she scratched his wide head, then dropped to her heels to extend the same favor to Oscar. She glanced around herself at the tiny, cramped space she inhabited and tried to envision where she'd put a crib.

"Stop it." She jerked to standing. "This is crazy. You're not pregnant."

But a powerful inner sense said different. She had no idea how early she could take a pregnancy test, yet some instinct chimed that one wasn't necessary.

"Don't borrow trouble," she ordered herself aloud to reinforce the message.

She could shout it, however; the tactic wasn't working. Now, more than ever, she wanted the cottage. Had to have the cottage. She would not bring up a child behind a bar.

Jezebel bent over the counter and dropped her head into her hands. How much more complicated could this get? If it was true, she would have to tell Gamble at some point, but how on earth would he take it?

Not well, she'd bet her life on that.

Would he insist on marrying her to provide—

"No." She straightened. Slapped her palms on the cracked tile to knock some sense into herself. "The condom only tore hours ago, and already you're getting married." She began to pace. To seek an answer to what to do, since inaction was never her first choice. She'd made a lot of mistakes in her life— dropping out of school, living on the streets, hooking up with lousy men—but she was beginning to correct them, and every step forward was the result of planning. The road out of the quagmire of her past had not been straight or smooth, but she had the money for a down payment because she'd thought ahead.

Maybe she wasn't pregnant. A part of her sighed and settled its shoulders in relief, though another piece of her mourned.

But if she was, then she had to plot very careful steps through the minefield that was Gamble Smith. The first one was to check with Levi to determine if her offer had been conveyed and if so, what Gamble's answer was. Whether she was pregnant or not, she still wanted that house, and somehow it seemed fitting that a child of his would grow up there. Not for a second did she consider an alternative to keeping any baby that might have resulted from last night.

And just in case, she poured out the coffee into the sink and began a cup of tea.

As she busied her hands, her mind ranged over what to do next. The small grocery in Three Pines wasn't open yet, and besides, she didn't dare buy a pregnancy test there. The news would be all over town before she pocketed her change.

At any rate, surely it was too soon to have answers to that question, but she could get another one resolved in the next hour or so when Levi's office hours began. Meanwhile, she couldn't stay here any longer; she'd wear the floor out pacing.

She could visit her cottage, however. Watch the sun rise.

And dream.

DAWN CREPT OVER the edge of the earth as Lily made her way to the first of her mother's three greenhouses that comprised the soul of Blossom Central. She longed to drive to the hospital and witness for herself what the nurse had conveyed: that her mother was resting comfortably, her condition was stable and no, she still had not awakened.

But Gamble was there, the woman told her. Had been most of the night. So Mama wasn't alone.

And she'd skin Lily if a single one of her plants died.

They're like babies, Marian Smith had always said. *Completely dependent on us for everything— food, water and light. We must give them the same devotion, Lily Belle. My babies are grown, and yours are still a ways off, so there's no good excuse for not tending these well, at least until your Prince Charming has come.*

Lily had worked beside her mother since she was small. Not forced effort—well, teenage tantrums excepted—but a labor of love that ran in her own blood, as well. From her earliest memories, Lily had relished having her hands in the dirt. She had a nose a winemaker would envy for its ability to divine the delicate chemistry in a sample of soil, what it lacked and what might be wrong. Roll it between finger and thumb, crumble it in her palm, then sniff and be on the mark every time…even her mother's wizardry could not compete with Lily's innate gift.

When she was younger, Lily imagined taking over the business and carrying on the tradition. There was only one cloud on the horizon.

Prince Charming didn't live in Three Pines and wasn't likely to visit.

As she watered and pinched, tamped soil gently over a stray root and rotated trays, Lily inhaled the peace that was as much a part of this rich, moist air as the tang of pine needles beneath her feet and spice of geraniums on her fingertips. And told herself that she was young yet and had plenty of years left.

But if anything happened to Mama—

No. Mama would be fine.

If anything did, though, the full weight of her mother's dream would press heavily on her shoulders.

And not for the first time, Lily wondered what she would be missing in the world outside Three Pines.

"Good mornin'."

Lily jolted. She hadn't heard the door open. "Hello, Calvin."

"You're up early. How's your mama?"

"Stable, they tell me." Deliberately, she didn't look up but kept working.

He halted beside her and lifted the spray nozzle from her hand, twisting it to the mist needed for the ferns hanging overhead. "I can finish here, *chère*. Bet you'd like to go visit her."

Tough, muscular Cal Robicheaux, sandy haired with wicked brown eyes, had the annoying habits of thinking he could read her mind and forgetting who gave the orders around here. Since he'd entered their lives three months ago as temporary help who seemed disinclined to leave, he'd taken on more and more responsibilities her mother had gladly handed over. Always respectful of Mama's opinions and tastes, he didn't accord Lily the same courtesy.

Mama thought he was the best thing since sliced bread. Lily thought he was a pain in the… Well, ladies didn't talk that way. And despite her frequently grimy fingernails and dirt-smeared jeans, Lily Belle Smith had been raised to be a Southern lady. She got back at him by calling him Calvin, a name he detested.

"Give me that." She held out a hand. "I finished the seedling house, but you can do the natives," she offered grudgingly, referring to the greenhouse where they cultivated only native species, kept apart from the others to prevent accidental cross-breeding.

"Wake up, sunshine. While you were in here dreamin', I already took care of them—and watered all the trees." He refused to relinquish the nozzle, but his voice softened. "You got plenty of reason to be preoccupied, *chère*. I went by the hospital on my way, and I'm aware that your mama ain't awake yet. I bet you didn't eat breakfast, either, did you?"

She grabbed a second hose. "Who are you? My—" At that, her voice faltered. She turned away quickly.

He stopped her with a hand on one arm. "You got to be worried sick, sugar, but starvin' yourself don't do anybody a bit of good." He abandoned his hold on her. "I brought you a couple of Lorena's cinnamon rolls. Might not be the best nutrition, but they'll go down easy. You head on inside, get yourself cleaned up and eat. I'll finish here and drive you over when you're done."

"Why are you being so nice to me?" she challenged. "I don't like you and you don't like me."

"Maybe not, but your mama gave me a chance when most people wouldn't, and I mean to do right by her." A half smile tilted the corners of his mouth. "Even if it includes dealing with her bossy daughter."

"I am not—"

He held up a hand. "I'm not arguing with you this

mornin', *chère*. You'd like nothin' better as a way to forget your worries, but your mama needs you, so just run along and do what you know is right."

"What's right is for me to watch over her nursery. She'd expect that."

"She'd also expect that she hired people to help, and they should be doing exactly that. I'll handle things today and however long I'm needed. You—" he pointed to the waterlogged trays beside her "—are too distracted."

Her eyes rounded in horror, then filled with tears.

He touched her shoulder. "They're mature enough that one day won't kill them. Now, go on inside, and I'll be there directly."

For a second, the temptation to lean against him nearly overcame her. Just in time, she shrugged him off and headed for the door. As she clasped the handle, she turned. "I can get myself to the hospital." Then she unbent. "But thank you for watching over things here. I'll be back as soon as I can. There's really nothing I can do to help her, but—"

"You never know, *chère*." He shook his head, then turned to his work. "You never know. Get on now."

For once, she had no ready retort waiting.

"Gamble?"

The touch on his arm jolted Gamble awake. "Wha—"

His sister's blue-gray eyes were soft and sad. "I thought you left to get some sleep. Why did you return?" She glanced over at their mother's bed. "The nurses said nothing had changed. Is there something they're not telling me?"

"No. I just—" He scrubbed at his face, not nearly ready to talk about his activities during the night. He'd driven here after he'd left Jezebel. He dropped his elbows onto his thighs and let his head hang, clearing his throat. "I wanted to be with her." He lifted his gaze to hers. "I haven't been around when she needed me."

Lily stroked his hair. "She understood why you left." Then she smiled. "She's thrilled about your success."

Gamble shrugged. "So people keep saying." He rose to pace. "I hate being here, Lily. What kind of jerk does that make me? Everything I loved was once in this town, and now I can't wait to leave." He saw her face crumple and realized what he'd said. "I'm sorry, Lily B. Of course there are still people I love here—you and Mom and Levi. And Noah's not that far. It's only that—" He stared out the window. "Everywhere I look, I see Charlotte. And being in a hospital again—"

"Mama wouldn't want you to be this miserable, Gamble."

He whirled. "She kept me alive all those months." He ground his teeth. "She never gave up on me. If you expect me to walk out on her simply because it's hard to be here—"

"When's the last time you had anything to eat?"

"What?" Images of onion rings and a hamburger led to inescapable images of Jezebel laid out on that same table as he'd bared her lush curves—

Gamble swore beneath his breath. Put his hands on his hips and squeezed his eyes to wring out the sight of her. Jezebel was an aberration, the night one he rued in the daylight. How in the hell, when his mother was lying here, helpless and alone and maybe dying, could he have—

"Gamble?"

"What?" he snapped.

Lily recoiled. "I only asked if you wanted to get some breakfast."

He raked his fingers through his hair. "No." Then he noted the hurt on her face. "I'm sorry. You're right. I should eat something."

"I read that bears emerging from hibernation are at their most dangerous," she teased, back to her normal sunny nature. "Come on, grouchy. Let's get that belly full of something nice."

"You won't be finding that in the cafeteria."

"We're not going to the cafeteria."

"I should catch Mom's doctor when he makes rounds."

"It's only six a.m., Gamble. He's not even out of bed yet." She smiled, showing the dimples that had been a cheerleader's pride and joy. "But we'll leave a cell number with the nursing station. Lorena's is only two blocks away."

Lorena's Café, where the biscuits could make a grown man weep. Suddenly, Gamble's stomach caught up with the game plan, rumbling to voice its opinion. He turned to his baby sister and saw her as the woman she'd become. "When did you get so relentless? You used to be just cute."

Her eyes sparked. "I was always relentless. Any girl with three big brothers has no choice." She dimpled again. "Cute is how a little sister gets things done."

Gamble found himself chuckling for the second time in twenty-four hours, though the women who'd provoked the laughter couldn't have been more diverse.

But he didn't want to think about Jezebel Hart anymore, so he grabbed his sister in a headlock and relished her squeal. "And this is how big brothers fight back."

A short scuffle ensued, as Lily sought to use her ultimate weapon: Gamble's ticklishness. He released the headlock and tried to dodge, but she was stuck on him like a tick, and those demonic fingers were everywhere. Short of really throwing his size against her, he was helpless, and Marian

Smith had taught her boys one cardinal rule: a man never takes advantage of a woman by virtue of being larger.

But his only other defense was to run from a girl he outweighed by a good eighty pounds, and a man had his pride.

Then inspiration hit. "Oh, no. Lily—check out your truck."

She hesitated just long enough for him to sweep her up and throw her over his shoulder.

"You creep!" Lily shrieked, and pummeled his back with her fists while Gamble laughed, belly-deep.

"What in blazes are you two doing? I swear I could hear you at the clinic."

Gamble faced Levi, as Lily struggled to right herself.

But both Levi and Noah, who was standing beside him, were grinning.

Finally, Gamble released Lily, who shoved an elbow into his belly. She shook her brown hair out of her eyes and huffed, "I was going to treat this big baboon to breakfast at Lorena's, but I've changed my mind."

Gamble sobered. "We should go back inside."

Noah's gaze flicked to the hospital entrance. "I just called a few minutes ago. They said Mom's condition hasn't changed."

"Yes, but—"

"Gamble was sleeping in the chair beside her

bed," Lily interrupted. "He needs to get away for a few minutes."

Gamble wasn't so certain. "I'll just go—"

"To breakfast with us," Levi said, and grabbed his arm. "Great idea, squirt."

Gamble gave one more glance back at the building.

"You're here, Gamble," Levi said quietly. "That's all she wanted. She's going to wake up, and she'll need help. None of us will be much good if we don't pace ourselves. You know she'd say the same thing."

Gamble paused, then exhaled. "You're right."

"Then it's settled." Noah grinned. "Lily's buying us all breakfast." He slung an arm around her neck.

"Guess again, fat cat. You're the one with the hot car. You pay."

"You're the one who was brawling in the parking lot in front of God and everybody."

"You are the most obnoxious—"

Gamble and Levi exchanged grins as the traditional bickering of their younger siblings heated up once more.

"Five dollars Lily wins," Levi observed.

"Sucker bet," Gamble answered. "He hasn't won an argument with her since she was ten, but okay." They shook hands. "Someone's got to prop up his ego."

AFTER A LOT of catching up and trading insults over coffee, they bent to the task of cleaning their plates once the food was delivered. Gamble couldn't remember enjoying a meal this much in years.

Suddenly, around the table, silence fell, and Gamble noticed them exchanging glances and braced himself.

Levi cleared his throat. "Would you two give us a minute?"

Lily glared, and Noah appeared relieved, already beginning to rise.

"Keep your seat," Gamble said. Then to Levi, "This is about the cottage, right?"

"Yeah."

"I'm not sure if I'm ready to sell it."

Levi exhaled sharply. "It's a good offer, Gamble. I promised the buyer an answer."

"What business do you have making promises about my house? And how can you say the offer's good when I never gave you a price?"

"Whoa, buddy," Noah cautioned. "You're out of line."

"It's my place. My sweat and blood that went into it. My decision and mine alone what to do with it and—"

"You ever plan to live there again?" Noah challenged.

"What concern is it of yours?" Gamble's gaze

swung around to each of them. "Any of you? If I get it in my head to let it rot to the ground, it's my own damn decision."

"Gamble." Lily placed one calming hand on his arm. "Levi's the one who's been watching over it more than any of us. You're not being fair."

She was right, but it didn't seem to matter. He shook her off and put his palms on the table's edge, prepared to depart. "I didn't ask anyone to do that."

"Sit down." Lily's voice could have been their mother's then, quiet but resolute. She caught his gaze and wouldn't let go. "It's a miserable topic, especially now, but that house deserves to be loved, Gamble. You put your heart and soul into it, and I don't believe you really want to see it crumble. God knows we all understand why you might never feel able to live there again, but you made it a piece of heaven, and Levi has someone who appreciates that. Who loves it precisely because she sees in it what you put there, board by board."

Gamble's anger deflated with Lily's words. His shoulders sagged. "I'm sorry. Noah's right—I was out of line."

Levi studied Gamble. "Sometimes I swear I'd sell my soul to love someone the way you loved Charlotte." He clapped Gamble on the shoulder. "Other times, I'm grateful as hell I don't. If you aren't ready to sell, fine, but if you don't plan to ever live here again, Lily's right—it's too great a place to just sit and rot. And Three Pines is hardly a hot spot for real estate. I can't imagine when you'd get a better offer."

"Part of me can't stand to ever set foot in it again. Another part can't forget—" Gamble rubbed his forehead, all at once as weary as he'd been in the middle of the night. "I don't know what I want to do, but give me the details and I'll think about it. Who's the buyer?"

"Her name is Jezebel Hart. She's managing Skeeter's Bar, but she says she's got savings enough for a down payment, and…"

His brother went on, but nothing penetrated the dull echo in Gamble's head.

Jezebel Hart. Dear God. Last night's mistake wasn't over after all. He'd thought when he left in the wee hours that he'd never see her again, that the insanity would remain safely buried because he'd soon be leaving and—

"Gamble?"

He finally noticed that all three of his siblings were eyeing him. "What?" He blinked. "I'm sorry. I—" He glanced away, then back. "No."

Levi frowned at him. "What do you mean, no? It's a fair price. You can't expect to do any better if you put it on the market—that is, if there were a real estate market in Three Pines—"

"No," he interrupted. "I'm not selling Charlotte's house to some floozy cocktail waitress." Even as he said the words, he winced inwardly, but only for a second. Selling Charlotte's house to a woman who just last night had fallen into bed with a perfect stranger was out of the question.

"She's not a waitress, not that it matters. Haven't you been listening to me? She's single-handedly saved Skeeter's bacon, and she's done some nice things for a number of people. She organized the—"

"I don't care." Gamble rose. "Tell her no."

Levi, too, stood. "Do it your own damn self. You explain why her money's not good enough." He was always slower to anger than Gamble, but when he finally got mad, it was not a sight for the faint of heart. "You've always been too saintly to darken Skeeter's door, but I'm sure you know the way." He threw down his napkin. "Or better yet, I'll drive you there myself and drop your haughty New York ass in the dirt."

"Would you two sit down?" Lily hissed. "People are staring. Maybe you don't care, but consider Mama."

The thought of embarrassing their mother drained the hot air out of them faster than anything else could. Gamble sat down with a sigh.

Levi didn't. "I'm done. I've got to open the clinic. I'll stop by the hospital later." He left without a backward look.

Gamble passed one hand over his face and cursed. "I can't explain." It was only partly a lie. His insides were a nasty mess of guilt and rage. "I'll square it with him somehow, but I can't…I'm not ready—"

"You don't have to decide just yet," Lily soothed. "Give it a few days."

Noah spoke up. "I met Jezebel, Gamble. Last time I was here. Don't assume too much from her name or what she does for a living."

Vivid images of that voluptuous body entwined with his made Gamble snort, even though the night was every bit as much his doing as hers.

"Go with me out there this evening, just to grab a beer. You can take her measure."

I already have, bro. I can still feel her hips in my hands, her thighs locked around—

He cleared his throat. "I don't think so."

"Why not? It isn't like you to be so close-minded, Gamble," Lily said. "Want me to come along?"

"No!" He was horrified at the mere idea.

"Mom says she's got a good heart. When she first came to town, people didn't know what to make of her, but she's generous with her time and—"

And her body. A sneer was building, but just then, a memory of her stroking his hair as he laid his head on her bosom intervened. The sense of comfort, of peace. He leaped to his feet. "I don't want to talk about it. I—"

"Hey, Gamble," said a voice from beside him.

He spotted Chappy Martinez and went very still.

"I was going to offer you a ride home last night from Skeeter's, but you and Jezebel seemed to have some business between you—"

That did it. Gamble turned from the gazes of his very interested siblings, threw some money on the table—

And stalked out the door.

CHAPTER SIX

GAMBLE HADN'T BOTHERED asking Noah if he wanted his car back. Sometime today, he'd go to his mom's nursery and see if that old truck of his dad's was still around; if not, he'd get someone to drive him to Tyler, where he'd rent a vehicle.

But for now, he needed to be alone.

And he had to face Charlotte's cottage.

Hell. He slapped his palm against the steering wheel. *Jezebel Hart thinks she deserves Charlotte's house.*

Of all the nerve—

An acid taste in the back of his throat was the perfect accompaniment to the tumult in his brain. He was furious. Outraged. Gut-sick with shame. He'd spent last night sitting in a third-rate bar, raking his gaze over that woman's flagrant curves, getting aroused by the thought of touching her, when Charlotte was dead in the ground and his baby with her. He'd never be able to touch his child's face or bury his nose in Charlotte's hair again. Never hold her close and protect her from—

Gravel sprayed, and the car spun as the tires lost purchase. For one tempting second, Gamble considered letting go. Allowing the embankment ahead—

He took control and skidded to a stop. His heart thudded as adrenaline rocketed through his blood.

He stared out the windshield and wondered why he'd stopped. Wasn't this what he'd wanted—to join Charlotte in that paradise she believed was waiting for them both?

He let his forehead fall onto the steering wheel and squeezed his eyes shut.

Paradise was out of his reach, had been ever since the day he'd railed at the sweet, frail woman who so fervently longed to bear his child. If there was such a place as heaven, she and the baby were surely there, since no one on earth had a purer heart.

But even if he hadn't let her die without his forgiveness, even if that grievous sin could somehow be expunged—

The fact that he'd fallen into bed with a bombshell instead of facing the home Charlotte had loved would surely spell his doom. And now he was supposed to hand over the keys of her dream to that same temptress and just… What? Walk away forever? Wipe out that part of his life?

Who would sit in Charlotte's rocking chair? Who would know that she treasured her grandmother's biscuit cutter? Understand how many nights she'd spent embroidering daisies on her kitchen curtains?

No. He couldn't sell the cottage. However desperate he was to escape the pain, it was his penance, his burden to bear. He had no right to move on, to forget her, though sometimes he wished he could just bash every memory out of his head. Once he'd had everything a man could wish for and had thrown heaven away.

Fantasies, he'd learned, carry a price, one he would never finish paying.

He pulled the car into the road and resumed his journey. Time for the next installment on his debt.

JEZEBEL ITCHED for a set of pruning shears. The trumpet vines tangling over this section of fence were about to topple it. She still knew too little about gardening, but beneath the tiny new leaves dusting the outer stalks lay a labyrinth of dead branches leaching once-white paint from the sweetly carved pickets. Surely some thinning out was in order.

If Marian Smith weren't in the hospital, she'd consult her. Her nursery brought customers from miles around to Three Pines because her stock was of the highest quality.

But Marian was in the hospital.

And she was Gamble's mother.

Under other circumstances, Jezebel thought, as she prowled the grounds of this place she longed to own, she would have joined the vigil, at least to the extent of running errands for Marian's children and friends or making coffee or snacks to help out.

But that was before last night.

She spotted a weed-choked flowerbed and dropped to her knees to lose herself in something productive.

What on earth would Marian think of her now? Jezebel had been celibate since her arrival, for months before that, as a matter of fact. Then, in one fell swoop, she'd laid eyes on Marian's grieving son—

And lost not only her mind but every shred of good sense she had.

Now here she was, all in an uproar, terrified that her life was irrevocably changed and—

"What the hell are you doing?" a voice roared.

Jezebel spun toward the intruder, lost her balance and fell smack on her behind in the mud.

Backlit by the rising sun's rays, a powerful, menacing frame towered over her. "Get off my property." The man's voice was guttural and fierce.

She shaded her eyes as she struggled to her feet—

And stared straight into the furious face of the man she most did not want to see.

He advanced on her. "You're trespassing. Beat it."

She backed into the rock edging and lost her

footing again. She grappled for something, anything, to catch her—

Instead, Gamble did.

The touch of this angry stranger had nothing in common with the eager, bone-melting caresses of last night or the man who'd leaped to her rescue. He gripped her arms so tightly she was sure she'd bruise.

"I'll give you thirty seconds, then I'm calling the sheriff." He squeezed harder, his face blazing with contempt. "I'll never sell this house to you, got that? You're not fit to wipe your shoes on Charlotte's mat. Get the hell out of here before I—"

Suddenly, she'd had enough. She used her own considerable strength to shove at his chest. "Take your hands off me, or I'll file charges for assault." When he didn't budge, she stomped her heel on his instep as she'd been taught in self-defense class.

He yelped, and his grip on her faltered. She slipped to the side while he hopped on one foot and cursed.

"Don't you dare manhandle me," she said.

If his face had been fury before, it settled into icy disdain now as he straightened. "Then don't ever let me find you here again. You don't belong. You never could."

Her racing heart twisted at the scorn in his tone. "You're letting this beautiful place fall into ruin. What kind of memorial is that?" The second her words were out, she wished she'd recalled them. She was not a hateful person.

But he'd made her feel worthless. For too long, that had been the story of her life.

"Get out." Visceral menace. "We're done."

She had the urge to laugh. *You might be surprised.* But she restrained herself, certain now that even if she were pregnant, she'd never tell him. She might not be worthy of much, but she merited more than his contempt. Even if she didn't, her baby did.

And for the sake of that child, she made herself speak up, though she craved to flee. "Tell me why."

He goggled. "What?"

"Why won't you sell it to me? You refuse to live in it."

"Because—" He flung out one hand and indicated the house. "If I were willing to sell Charlotte's house, it would never be to someone like you."

She steeled herself against the insult. "There were two people in that bed last night. I didn't notice any restraints being used."

He recoiled. "It was a mistake."

The return barb nailed its mark with devastating aim. A night that she couldn't forget, he called only a mistake.

The child she prayed she wasn't carrying…was a mistake.

No. "You're wrong."

His head jerked upward. His eyes could have melted steel. He didn't want to remember the tenderness; she understood that now. Didn't want any part of kindness, wished for nothing at all from her, really.

But she craved something from him, so she forced herself to breathe deeply and try once more. "Gamble," she began. "I realize that it's painful for you to be here—"

"You understand nothing. Someone like you couldn't begin to—"

She drew herself up. "Shut up. Stop treating me like dirt because you feel guilty that you got your rocks off last night." *No, no, no—get a grip.* She exhaled. Fought for calm. "I'm sorry. That was unkind."

"Just go." He turned his back.

"I'll leave, out of respect for how much you loved her, but you ponder something after I'm gone." His head was in motion, already shaking her off, but she refused to let him deter her. "Ask yourself this, Gamble Smith—what would Charlotte do? If she couldn't stand being here because it hurt too much without you, would she let all the love in this place go to waste? Because I love it, whether or not you believe I'm worthy, and I'd do my best to care for what you and Charlotte built."

He rounded on her. "You didn't know Charlotte,"

he growled, "and you don't know me." He jabbed one finger toward her car. "And you're on my property."

She remained when she longed to run, though tears blinded her eyes.

Then, when she felt she'd proved her point, she made her way out of what could have been paradise.

ONCE SHE WAS GONE, Gamble sagged to the porch steps, drained by the fury that never seemed to fully leave him.

What would Charlotte do?

That cut deep.

None of your business, bimbo.

But even as he thought it, he wondered at himself. Charlotte would never tear around like a rampaging bull; that was for sure. She would not aim to hurt someone who didn't deserve it.

But she hurt me. *She left* me. The insidious voice taunted him, the same demon that had sucked the marrow out of him in those lost months after her death.

He forced himself to his feet to escape its lure. To fight another spiral down into that pit of despair.

Then face it. Her house. Your house. Home.

He shook his head violently. This wasn't his home, not anymore.

So why can't you sell it?

Because—

He couldn't explain it. His feelings about this

place were a vicious tangle of love and hate and lost hope. He couldn't separate the pain from the love. Couldn't be here and not remember—

Gamble, take a break. Come swing with me. His eyes moved inexorably toward the porch swing he'd built and hung for her, just where she could sit and watch the sun set. Laughing eyes and welcoming arms. *Let's snuggle.*

And he had, so many times. He'd awaken to find her bundled up in her grandmother's wedding-ring quilt on a brisk morning, gaze fastened on a mockingbird singing to greet the day. Or with a pitcher of fresh-squeezed lemonade waiting for him, its rounded sides beaded with moisture against a sweltering summer afternoon.

Or sitting in his lap in the moonlight, drowsy and replete with sweet passion.

Another image speared into his brain at that moment: a woman as different from Charlotte as blazing sun is from cool starlight. Abundant curves and no-holds-barred sex, her eyes daring him to leap from a cliff and discover just how wild the ride could be, until he'd lost his mind right along with her.

Just the thought of it had lust curling in his gut.

Gamble slammed his palm against a post. Here, in Charlotte's domain, the mere idea of another woman was unconscionable. He'd never been unfaithful to her, never even considered it. If their lovemaking had had to be more careful and had required him to rein himself in, such was a price he had paid gladly.

Don't be so careful with me, Gamble. I won't break.

But she'd been wrong, no matter how much she'd wished otherwise. She hadn't been the one forced to walk the floor at night, trying to decide if this spell would worsen or fade, who must calculate when they could weather the crisis and when it was too dangerous not to haul her back to the hospital where too many hours of her life had passed.

He'd do it all again, gladly, in exchange for that oasis she'd supplied, that place where his restless spirit had found such peace. Not many people got to live with an angel, and few deserved it less than Gamble Smith.

If she couldn't stand being here because it hurt too much without you, would she let all the love in this place go to waste?

No. She wouldn't. But Charlotte was the angel, not him.

He glanced around and noticed, for the first time, the true price of his neglect. Being here was making him crazy; until his mother's fate was known, though, he couldn't leave, however badly he craved to.

First things first. Noah would be ready for his car, and Gamble owed an apology to his siblings. However deeply mixed were his feelings about selling, that was no excuse for jumping down Levi's throat.

Gamble scanned his surroundings and made a silent promise to return. His gaze paused on the flowerbed Jezebel had been weeding, mud on her long, graceful fingers and on the back of the curve-hugging jeans.

His body, damn him, still responded to her. Would say yes again in a heartbeat, if offered.

Except the house stood between them now.

He wanted out of Three Pines desperately. He couldn't wait to get back to New York.

For the moment, though, that wasn't an option, so he'd go to the hospital to check on his mother, then make the rounds of his siblings and eat crow.

And pray that the day of his departure wasn't far off.

CAL WAS KNEE-DEEP in pine mulch when Lily returned, working alongside sixteen-year-old Kenny Davis to fill the bags that bore Mama's signature label—scarlet rosebuds surrounding the script Blossom Central. It was dusty work, so he wore a bandanna over his nose.

"I told you to use a mask."

He glanced up but kept shoveling. "I like this better."

"You're just too vain to wear one."

He lowered the bandanna, leaned on the shovel and winked at Kenny. "What did I tell you? The woman can't resist me."

Lily rolled her eyes. "You've sucked too much dust up your nostrils. It's clogged your brains."

Instead of an answering insult, he squinted at her, then handed the shovel to Kenny. "Take five, kid."

Kenny grinned. "It's more fun watching you two."

Cal ruffled his hair. "You'll get other chances, I'm sure. Scram."

Kenny complied, emerging from the pile with his usual gawkiness.

"Wait," Lily said. "Why aren't you in school?"

"I told him to ditch."

"You what?" She whirled on Cal. "Calvin, you have no right—"

Kenny started laughing. "It's okay, Lily. We have a teacher in-service day."

"Spoilsport," Cal said. "Beat it. But be back in ten minutes. We got fifty bags to fill yet."

"Slave driver." Kenny waved as he walked away.

"You're a terrible influence on that impressionable boy," she complained. Kenny had a serious case of hero worship.

"Ever'body oughta have an example not to follow." He stopped before her, his eyes too assessing. "What's wrong, *chère?* Your mama okay?"

She shrugged. "No worse, but no better."

"Thought she might like to have her own flowers around her. Maybe the scent of them might bring her back, if for nothin' more than to chew my ass out for cuttin' her precious blooms."

Lily had to smile. "She will, too. I'll go arrange them."

He ducked his head. "Already did."

She blinked. "You? Created a bouquet?"

"What's the big deal? You cut some stems, stick 'em in a vase."

"Which blooms?" Lily was already charging toward the workroom. "Calvin, the Nichols wedding is next weekend. If you've raided the flowers Mama has been coddling for months and get Gladys Nichols riled, I swear I'll—"

His shout of laughter brought her up short.

"It's not funny. I can't leave you for a minute, can I?" She spun on her heel, ready to rip into him.

He intercepted the finger she was about to jab at him. "But you're not sad anymore, are you, *chère?*" He released her and stepped back. "I'd rather see you spitting mad. Your mama needs you to fight, not cry over her. She's tough, and she's gonna come out of this just fine, you watch. Now, some of us got to work around here." He parted ways at the workroom door.

Just before he moved out of hearing, she spoke up. "So did you pick Mama's blossoms or not?"

He paused. "I'll leave that up to you, sugar. But you gotta admit, it's a good idea." He saluted and left.

"Good idea, my foot." But she was smiling as she reached for the door handle.

"Lily. Ms. Smith."

She looked over her shoulder. Went very still. "Ms. Hart." She'd never decided quite what she thought of the woman, despite her mother's rapport with her. Now, on the heels of Gamble's reaction and the shocking news that he'd been with Jezebel last night, Lily found herself speechless.

Furious, actually. How dare this woman set her sights on Lily's grieving brother? Whatever resignation Lily had felt about Jezebel wanting the cottage evaporated into pure steam. "Can I help you?" she said without welcome.

Jezebel towered over Lily, but at the moment, she seemed smaller. Uncertain. "I—" She glanced around as if seeking help. She wore a perfectly ordinary white T-shirt tucked into worn jeans, yet Lily couldn't help peering down at herself, dressed nearly the same but without any of the flair. She had about as many curves as Kenny, while Jezebel in a gunnysack would still be a raving beauty and stop male hearts wherever she went.

Which made it even more reprehensible that Jezebel had used the stun force of her body to hijack Gamble into God knows what foolishness.

"I have a lot of work to do," Lily snapped.

Jezebel recoiled. "I'm sorry. Of course you'd be busy with your mother gone. I stopped by the hospital to check on her just now. I'd like to get her some flowers."

"Why?"

The woman seemed startled. "Your mother has always been so nice to me. I care about her." Her eyes glistened. "You must be worried sick. If there's anything I can—"

"I think you've done enough."

"What?"

"Don't play the innocent. What happened—you decide to ensure the sale by seducing my brother?"

Jezebel's reaction could not have been more telling.

"Oh, no." Lily felt sick. "You did. You honestly took advantage of a man who's heartsick over the only woman he'll ever love, just so you could buy the house he built for her."

"I didn't—"

Lily advanced on her. "You make me want to puke. Of all the lowdown, lousy things to do. My mother may be fooled by you, but I'm not. It figures that a stripper would come up with a tactic like that. You and your No Profanity jar and your meals for the lonely—you're a fraud, aren't you? Men can't see past that overblown figure of yours, but that won't work on me, I assure you." All the horror of her impotence to bring her mother back to them coalesced into the certainty that here was something she could do: shield her brother from this conniving seductress. "Go away and don't return. We don't need your money, and my mother only felt sorry for you. And if you ever come near my brother again, I'll make you wish you hadn't."

"Lily." Cal's voice from behind her, sharp with command. "Stop."

She yanked her attention from Jezebel and pounced on him. "Don't you tell me what to do. You're no better than she is. As a matter of fact, you'd fit together just right—an ex-con and a not-so-ex-stripper. Why don't the two of you just get out of my sight and go—"

Cal gripped her arms and shook her gently. "She's gone, Lily. Quit this. She's not who you're mad at."

She slammed a clenched hand into his chest. "Don't you tell me what I'm feeling. And if you insist on taking her side, then you can just pick up your check, you hear me?" She struggled to get away from him, to no avail.

"I'm not going anywhere but to drive you to the hospital."

Lily froze, terrified to look at him and see what he meant. "Oh, God. What's wrong with Mama?"

But when she did, he was smiling. "She did some-thin' real, real right." He touched one finger to her chin. "Your mama decided to wake up, *chère*."

"Oh, Cal." Lily burst into tears.

"Forgot to call me Calvin." He turned her and began to lead her to the car. "You're definitely too shook up to drive."

CHAPTER SEVEN

GAMBLE HAD WHEELED into the nursery parking lot just in time to witness his sister struggling in the grip of a man he'd never met. He bolted from the car. "Take your hands off her." Behind him, he barely registered the sound of Noah's cell phone ringing.

Lily wheeled in his direction and registered his intent. "Gamble, no—"

She was too late. His fist caught the guy's jaw with a satisfying crack. The impact sang up Gamble's arm; the man was nearly his height and solid muscle.

His opponent braced for combat, and Gamble welcomed the release of a good fight.

"No!" Lily leaped at Gamble and clung to his right arm.

He attempted to shake her off.

"Gamble, listen, you hard-headed baboon. He's not hurting me."

"You were fighting to get away."

"Calvin was only trying to make me see reason."

The man she called Calvin stood ready, but his mouth quirked in a grin. "Don't know why I bother, *chère*," he drawled.

"Shut up," Lily said, and turned to Gamble. "If I let go, will you listen to me for a second? There's something more important than Calvin to discuss."

"Sugar, you wound me."

Gamble narrowed his gaze at the stream of endearments. "What's he to you?"

Lily tossed her head. "Nothing."

Calvin slapped a hand to his chest. "Now, that's just low." But his eyes danced.

Gamble relaxed, couldn't help a chuckle. "And here I was hoping for a fight." He held out a hand. "Calvin, I'm Gamble Smith."

"Call me Cal. Robicheaux. Only Lily Belle here insists on irritatin' me with the full name."

"She takes irritation to an art form."

"Tell me about it." They clasped hands and grinned.

"Men. You're all idiots." Lily stepped between them and grabbed Gamble's arms. "But forget that. Gamble, Mama's awake."

"What? Why didn't anyone tell me?"

"Didn't I hear Noah's cell ringing?"

Gamble opened his mouth to deny it, and closed it just as quickly. "Probably. I thought he was hurting you so—"

Lily pressed her hands to his cheeks. "My hero." She smirked at Cal. "Don't mess with me, Calvin. I have big brothers at my beck and call."

Gamble hooked an arm around her neck and gave her a noogie. "Yeah, yeah, yeah. Come on, pest. Let's split." He glanced back at Cal. "You riding with us?"

The look the man bestowed on Lily told Gamble that there was more at work here than simple irritation, but Cal only shrugged. "No, you go ahead. I'll watch over things here. Give Miz Marian my best."

JEZEBEL PASSED the hospital on her way to the nursing home and pondered stopping off there first. Just as quickly, she rejected the idea, still stinging from the reactions of Gamble and Lily. Levi might be more welcoming, but he was probably at his clinic, and she only knew Noah by sight. Maybe the best thing she could do for a woman she admired was to steer a wide berth around Marian's children.

She pulled into the parking lot of the nursing home and was gratified to see Skeeter sitting under the portico, relishing the glory of a sweet spring day. He waved, and she paused a minute to gather herself and shake off the morning's unpleasantness.

With a deep breath, she emerged from the car and retrieved the brownies she'd baked. She pasted on the smile that Skeeter deserved and headed up the sidewalk.

"Hi there, handsome." She bent and kissed his cheek. "What brings you outside?" The nursing staff was as worried as she was that Skeeter kept to his room so often. "Trolling for the ladies?" she teased.

"Hmmph." But he favored her with a wink. "Waitin' for my getaway car, more like. Women 'round here about to drive a man crazy with all their flutterin' and fussin'."

How she wished she could provide that getaway vehicle, but she had nowhere to take him. Even if he were completely healed, he couldn't live alone and might never be able to do so again. The quarters behind the bar were too cramped, and he'd refused to consider letting her sleep on the couch as she'd offered previously.

Now Gamble Smith had flatly rejected her offer to buy the place she had her heart set on making into a home for this man who was the only paternal figure she'd had in many years.

She'd figure out something; she always did. And Skeeter could use cheering, not sharing her gloom. "It must be terrible having all the ladies vying for your favor. Most men wouldn't be complaining."

"Neither would I if they weren't a bunch of ninnies," he groused.

"What about Mary Faith?"

Skeeter went a most intriguing shade of pink. "Don't know what you're talkin' about."

She snickered. "Liar." She pressed a kiss to his cheek. "You Casanova, you."

"Here now, young lady, I don't have to take your guff. Set your impertinent fanny down and tell me how things are going at the bar."

She settled beside him and nearly wept at the feel of sun on her face. The sound of…quiet. She closed her eyes and soaked it in. Not silence, really—a bird warbled atop the magnolia to the left of the drive. Wind shirred through the stand of live oaks dotting the lawn. A squirrel skittered across the roof, and in the distance, a plane engine droned. Now and again, a car passed on Main Street, tires hissing on the blacktop.

Hustle and bustle, Three Pines-style.

To her endless surprise, she couldn't get enough of it.

"You want a nap, feel free. My bed's empty."

She blinked. Stirred. "Sorry."

He focused all-knowing eyes on her. "You can't keep burning the candle at both ends, little girl."

Little girl. She couldn't help grinning. She topped Skeeter by half a foot, minimum. "I'm doing fine."

"You can't lie worth a damn."

She tucked away everything but what was best for

the man beside her. "Hard work never killed anyone."
She winked. "Keeps me out of the pool hall."

It was his turn to snort. "I'll be up and around any
day now. Then you can become a lady of leisure."

"Of course you will." But her heart quailed.
What would she do if he truly didn't need her?
Even if Russ Bollinger wasn't a threat, she'd come
to like the sense of belonging, however tenuous,
she felt here.

Then she pictured Lily Smith's face. *My mother
may be fooled by you, but I'm not.* Gamble would
leave again soon, but Lily would remain. Marian had
welcomed Jezebel, but Lily was not without her influence. If she decided to ostracize Jezebel, she
would win.

Don't borrow trouble, Jezebel's long-dead mother
had told a little girl prone to worry.

Jezebel forcibly relegated Gamble and Lily and
the future to the back of her mind. "Oscar sends his
love," she said, knowing that would set Skeeter off.

"A cat in my place." He said the word *cat* as if it
were the vilest of curses. "What did I say about
women being trouble?" But he grinned at her. "Tell
ol' Rufus to chomp a bite outta that feline's behind for
me. Now, catch me up on the bar. Louie still moonin'
over you? And what's this I hear about ferns?"

Jezebel grinned. "Chappy's been by, I guess?"

"Yeah, but he don't tell stories worth a durn. Start with Darrell."

She leaned back in her chair and began to talk.

"WHY DOES CAL have to make you see reason?" Gamble asked Lily, simply to break up the ponderous silence as they both contemplated what sort of shape their mother would be in.

"A little disagreement over a customer, that's all." She averted her face, but color stained her cheeks.

"Like what?"

"Nothing important." But she still wouldn't look at him.

She was probably remembering his behavior earlier. "Lil, I owe you an apology."

"Me? Why?"

He lifted a shoulder. "You know. At the café. I was a jerk about the house, and none of you deserved that. It's just…hard."

Her eyes went soft. She touched his forearm. "You loved her so much. I'm with Levi. Sometimes I envy you, but other times—" She studied her lap. "I'm not sure if it's worth what you've gone through."

Unexpectedly, Gamble's eyes stung. Would he give up the years with Charlotte just to avoid what he felt now? With a sigh, he glanced at his sister.

"Someone asked me what Charlotte would do if our positions were reversed."

Lily's eyebrows lifted, but she didn't push him for an answer.

Gamble peered out the windshield. "She'd handle it better than I have, that's for sure. She was always the better person. Much more than I deserved."

"You're wrong about that," Lily said. "You treated her like a princess. She told me once that every woman should have a knight in shining armor like she did. You made her so happy, Gamble."

"Then why—" He clamped his mouth shut. He was all too cognizant of Charlotte's reasoning for bearing his child. But he still couldn't forgive it, and he couldn't admit that to a soul. Especially not a younger sister who thought their story was so romantic.

"Why what?"

"Never mind." He was desperate for a change of topic. "So what did this customer do that got you and Cal at odds?"

"She just—" Lily paused. Then mutiny chased over her features. "I can't believe that hussy had the nerve to take advantage of you, Gamble. To seduce you to get you to agree to sell the cottage is the lowest thing I've ever heard."

Gamble fumbled the wheel as he pulled into the

hospital parking lot. His mind reeled as he found a space and parked.

"Jezebel was at the nursery?" Was Lily right about what she'd done? Just as quickly as he wondered, he rejected that explanation. Jezebel hadn't known his name when she'd first started flirting with him—had she?

He'd had a lot to drink that night, and his memory was clouded. Was that what she'd had in mind all along, to somehow use that knockout body to soften him up for her offer to buy the cottage?

Well, it backfired, Ms. Hart. Big-time.

"She had the nerve to come in to buy some flowers for Mama—doesn't that beat all? I set her straight, I promise you that. No gold digger is going to seduce my brother, then cozy up to our mother when seduction fails."

Conflicting images tore at him—Jezebel tempting him to play, promising only one night of no-strings sex.

Cotton underwear and her arms crossed over her chest. Her offer to let him go home when he lost his nerve.

The laughter, then the blinding heat of her body, entwined with his. The sense of connection for those brief moments after—

A hand slapped the hood. Gamble jolted, then saw Noah's face.

Grinning. Levi beside him, just as happy.

"How is she?" Lily leaped from the car. "Is she talking to you? What does the doctor say?"

"Whoa there, Lily B." Noah held up his palms. "One question at a time." But his humor was an answer in itself.

"She's going to be okay." For the first time in two days, Gamble drew a deep breath.

"She's not out of the woods yet, but the doctor is optimistic. She's got a long recovery ahead—" His face split in a wide smile. "She already asked when we're rescheduling the party."

Lily's eyes teared up.

Levi spoke. "With several more days in the hospital, at a minimum, then a lot of physical therapy once the break heals, Mom isn't going dancing any time soon."

"But she'll be home," Lily said. "She'll be all right."

"A lot's going to fall on you, Lily B," Levi said. "It could be months before she's completely well."

"I don't care. I just want her back where she belongs."

"I'll do everything I can. Noah has to return to his job, and Gamble will be returning to New York." Levi raked his fingers through his hair. "After I close the clinic at night, I can spell you, but there's still the nursery to deal with. Margins are too thin to hire much more help, aren't they?"

"I'll stay." The words were out before Gamble could think.

Relief chased over Levi's face, followed by a frown echoed in Lily's expression. "Your career is just getting off the ground. And what about your place there? From what I hear, New York real estate is way too expensive to be paying rent when you're not around."

Gamble didn't have any good answers; he dreaded staying in Three Pines one second longer than he must, but they'd always pulled together as a family in the past, and he'd shouldered too little of his share since Charlotte died. "We'll figure out details later. I just—" He shrugged. "My work is portable, and I can sublet, if it comes to that. Noah can help on weekends." He glanced over at his youngest brother, who nodded. "And we'll make it work out. You two shouldn't be penalized just because you live in town."

Levi still seemed troubled. "Gamble, Mom wouldn't ask—"

"Mom needs our help. Enough said." Gamble clapped his hand on Levi's shoulder. "And you don't always have to carry the weight of the world just because you're the eldest." From somewhere he found a grin to cover his dread. "Anyway, you're not the boss of me." The reference to an old refrain had them all chuckling.

"So…let's go welcome Mom back to the land of the living."

Lily launched herself into Noah's arms and dragged Gamble and Levi close, too. The four of them clung in a hug of thanksgiving, and Gamble put away his questions about Jezebel Hart and her motivations for now.

Arm in arm, they strode into the hospital, and for the first time in years, Gamble was looking forward to a visit to a medical floor.

JEZEBEL PICKED UP the pregnancy test again. Set it down with a thud. Unfolded the instructions once more, but nothing in them had changed.

She had to wait until her first skipped period to be sure. "I thought they said early," she muttered. "Early is now. Yesterday, not four days."

Oscar leaped to the toilet seat and butted her hand with his head.

"What if I'm not in the mood to pet?"

He rubbed her fingers and purred.

She dropped to her heels in front of him and buried her fingers in his fur with a sigh. "What am I going to do?" she whispered. Rufus stuck his cold nose on her arm and she lost her balance. Collapsed on her behind.

Then her arms were full of dog. She clasped him

to her and held on. "What on earth do I do?" she repeated.

Took advantage of a man who's heartsick over the only woman he'll ever love...my mother only felt sorry for you. Lily's contempt had been clear.

You're not fit to wipe your shoes on Charlotte's mat. Gamble's fury.

It would be so easy to pack up and run. So tempting.

But Skeeter's eyes were losing their hope, and she was sick to death of landing in places that would never be home.

Jezebel gave the dog one last ruffle of fur, the cat an additional stroke, then rose to her feet and stared in the mirror. "You've run too often, Jezebel Hart, but not this time." She started the shower to get ready for work. "Some people are just going to have to learn that lesson the hard way."

CHAPTER EIGHT

WHEN DARRELL ARRIVED, Jezebel already had all the chairs down off the tables, the glassware sparkling, lemons and limes sliced and the small bowls of fiery peanuts set out. She had cheese heating for nachos and chips already in the warmer, and she was measuring the windows.

"Uh-oh," he said. "What's wrong?"

"Hello to you, too," she replied airily. "Why would you think something's wrong?"

He removed a fresh apron from the drawer and donned it. "Maybe because when you're upset, you start redecorating. Folks barely survived the fern. Don't you even consider bringing any frilly curtains in here, girl. I'll go drag Skeeter's ass back, prop him up in a bed in the corner, if I have to. Somebody got to rein you in now and again."

He was grinning, but she couldn't return his humor. The mention of Skeeter was a barb beneath her skin, highlighting her failure to salvage anything of her dreams from this thoroughly miserable day.

"Hey—I was only fooling with you. Didn't mean to make you cry."

She tossed back her hair. "I'm not crying. I'm fine." She glanced around them for some distraction. "Maybe I'll—"

Darrell caught her arm, murder in his eye. "What did that sonofabitch do to you?" He reached for the strings of his apron and wheeled around. "Don't matter. I get a piece of him, regardless."

"Darrell, I'm okay."

He whirled to face her. "Oh, yeah, I can tell how happy you are. Shoulda known the second I walked in the door why you got that long face and those big, sad eyes." His brows slammed together. "Not that I didn't warn you, oh, no. Did I warn you he was bad news? 'Course I did, but would you listen?" He slapped the apron on the bar and stalked to the back door.

"Stop—" she called to him. "Please. I need you here and—" To her relief, he finally faced her. "He didn't do anything I didn't want him to do." Gamble had exceeded her expectations physically; the man was indeed a very gifted lover.

No, it wasn't their interlude that was the problem; it was everything after. The broken condom, his reaction to her presence at the cottage. His sister's accusations she hadn't bothered trying to refute. The awareness that she'd let Skeeter down.

Drained by the overload of emotions today, she settled into a chair and rubbed one thumb over the tabletop.

Darrell paused beside her, still stiff with outrage. "Jez, I will gladly kick his tail from here to South Carolina for you. I can't stand seeing you look so defeated. That ain't like you. The man's bad news. He comes in this door again, and I will make him pay, I assure you." He crouched beside her. "Why don't you go home. Take the night off. You're beat. I can run things, and if I get too busy, I'll recruit Louie to help."

"Oh, my word." She shoved to her feet. "Now you're trying to scare me." He stood, too, and she found a smile for him. "You're a good friend, Darrell. The big brother I never had." She squeezed his arm. "I'm all right, I promise. And working's the best thing for me now." She moved past him and paused. "As for Gamble Smith, he won't be around here anymore, but I thank you for volunteering to be my champion."

"Three Pines ain't big enough for him to hide. I will have words with him, Jezebel."

"You will not. I forbid you."

His eyebrows rose into his hairline. "Shirley would tell you that giving me orders seldom pans out."

Jezebel found a grin. "Want me to ask her about that?"

He waved her off. "I'm just saying. But I don't suppose you gonna listen to me any better than she does." He snagged his apron from the nearby table and stalked into the kitchen, muttering.

Jezebel found her heart a little lighter from the simple fact of his caring. She'd been alone and drifting for years now, and the idea of having friends rally around warmed her. Every once in a while, she got restless from sheer habit, probably, but what a luxury it was to have people with whom you had a history. She would soon begin her second year of knowing people like Darrell and Louie and others, and she still got a little thrill each time she experienced a small echo of a past and a future in the same place. The simplest things, such as having a memory of last Thanksgiving and anticipating what would be the same this November and what might not…that resonance of past with future, that unbroken thread leading from then to now—she had the urge to seize each connection and hold on tight, lest it be snatched away.

She stood in the middle of Skeeter's bar and realized that soon the space would be crowded with people she knew, with laughter and stories and irritation and, God willing, curses to fill her jar…and she would be there tonight as she had been last night…as she would tomorrow night—

Jezebel squared her shoulders and rubbed at a smudge on the tabletop. Maybe she would never get that cottage, though she certainly hadn't given up yet…even so, she would be here tomorrow and tomorrow and tomorrow—

And Gamble Smith would be long gone. Back in New York and faded from memory. She would never have to see him again, if she was lucky.

But what if I'm pregnant?

She wasn't. She couldn't be.

But if you are?

"Hey, Jez." The front door opened, and Louie stepped inside. Right behind him was Chappy. "Can a man get a cold beer around here after a long day's work?"

"Get real." Chappy snorted. "Last time you did a day's work I was in diapers."

The affectionate bickering began, and Jezebel had no more opportunity for thoughts of Gamble or babies or cottages.

She threw her arms around Louie's neck and gave him a big, smacking kiss on the cheek, leaving a vivid red imprint from her lipstick.

"What was that for?" But his face glowed with pleasure.

"Just for fun," she responded as she rounded the bar to get them their drinks.

GAMBLE FINISHED CLEANING the kitchen after supper. As he loaded the dishwasher, he stared out the window, lost in thought.

It was so quiet here; he'd forgotten that. Had to, or Manhattan and its constant din would have driven him out of his mind.

Lily was gone; he prowled the house where he'd grown up, picking up a photo here, a knickknack there. Reminders of a life that seemed both real and distant. New York felt as faraway as if it had never happened.

Then he spied a clipping his mother kept beside her chair: Kat, in all her blazing glory, the night she'd tried to lure him to her bed to celebrate the stupendously successful opening of his show.

And he beside her, his insides a mess. He'd been sick to death of the simpering crowd, all eager to discuss the deeper meanings of his art, the message beneath.

While he'd been ready to rip every painting off the wall or howl at the moon because all he could think was how empty the victory was without Charlotte beside him. That he was doing exactly what she'd always dreamed for him hadn't helped.

That he was alive and she was dead—he hadn't been able to see beyond that. He'd been half-blind with the need to escape and run back—

Gamble tossed the clipping on the table. There'd been nothing to run back to. He grabbed the remote and flipped through channels and channels of nothing. He turned off the television. Propelled himself to standing and paced again.

Wished Noah hadn't had to return to Dallas on business.

Go with me out there this evening. Take her measure.

I can't believe that hussy had the nerve to take advantage of you.

He paused, hands on hips, and tried to square the many faces of Jezebel Hart. A schemer or just out for a good time? But he remembered her affection for Louie and Chappy and others at the bar. *They come for family.*

Who was she, beneath it all?

Then Gamble knew exactly where he was going tonight.

THE NOISE HIT HIM before he opened the door—boisterous laughter, affectionate jeers. The click of pool balls barely heard above a raucous country song on the jukebox.

He shoved open the wood and entered.

And there she was.

Sultry was the first word that leaped to mind. She was in jeans again, tight enough to have been painted on those hips that were meant to be held in a man's hands.

He could still feel them in his.

Her blouse, a royal blue this time, plunged to a vee between those stunning breasts, wrapped across her midriff and tied at the waist in a big floppy bow. Every time she moved, a slice of ivory skin taunted him. She moved a lot.

Blue-and-silver dangles winked at her ears amid the profusion of black curls tumbling over her shoulders and down her back. She'd caught some of her hair up to reveal the curve of one perfect ear and an enticing sweep of throat.

On her arms, bangles sparkled. The long line of her endless legs topped feet encased in black high-heeled sandals, revealing carmine toenail polish.

Man, she made his mouth water.

"You get the hell out now, you hear me?" Darrell broke into Gamble's line of sight, fury on his face. "Your money's no good here, not after what you did to her."

Gamble blinked. "Me? I didn't—" Then his gaze fell on the table of the booth where he'd spread her out like a feast.

Darrell shoved him. "You turn around and walk away, or I throw your ass out in the dirt."

Gamble's hands clenched. "Maybe you should ask her what really happened."

Darrell's nostrils flared. His frame tensed, his arm cocked to—

"Darrell, please go back to the bar." Jezebel stepped between them, her voice low. In her heels, she was nearly as tall as the two men she was trying to part. Gamble couldn't peer past the wild mane to tell how Darrell was reacting, but he didn't appreciate the interruption.

"Jez, step aside," Darrell said.

Around them a crowd was gathering.

"Darrell, I know you mean well, but everything's already too rowdy tonight. Skeeter can't afford any broken furniture, and if you two start fighting, it will escalate. I'll just escort Mr. Smith to the door, and everything will settle down." She placed a hand on his arm. "Please."

Darrell cast Gamble a glare that promised retribution. "Don't waste your time on this lowlife, Jez. He ain't worth one more tear."

Startled, Gamble peered at Jezebel. She'd cried?

Her body language said that she was displeased with the revelation. "One round on the house," she called out. A small cheer rose.

Darrell backed off reluctantly and made for the bar.

Jezebel's features were schooled into neutrality. "I would appreciate it if you'd go."

"We have to talk first." He noted an instant of panic and wondered at it.

"We have nothing to discuss."

So close to her, he could smell her perfume, something spicy and floral mixed with the scent he already recognized as solely hers: lush, ripe woman. He scanned her figure, and his body responded powerfully.

He should leave now. But he couldn't.

Was she doing this on purpose? Scrambling his brains with sex? Sweet mercy, she exuded clouds of it, blurring his ability to recall why he was here.

Except that he'd had to.

"Please leave." Her tone was flat.

Gamble shook his head to clear it and blurted out the first thing that came to mind. "My mother's awake."

Her eyes widened. "I'm glad. How is she?"

"Fragile. So small it scares you to death."

She warmed a bit. "She's a strong lady."

Someone bumped her, and Gamble steadied her. He didn't remove his arm.

"She always has been, but now—"

Sympathy bloomed in her expression. "I understand. Some days Skeeter breaks my heart." She hesitated. "Look—" She glanced around, then seemed to reach a reluctant decision. "Let's step outside. It's too noisy in here."

She surveyed the group. "I'll be in the parking lot. No swearing while I'm gone. Chappy, you collect the money for me if there is."

Chappy perked up. Louie grumbled.

But nobody argued.

Gamble caught Darrell's scowl but ignored it and followed her.

But once outside, it was too quiet. Too dark and... intimate. He didn't know why he was here anymore.

She rescued him. "What do the doctors say?"

"That's it's going to be a long haul for her. She should recover, and her mind seems intact, despite the coma."

"That's a good sign, isn't it?"

"Yeah." He swiped a hand over his hair. "But she's got months of physical therapy ahead, and Lily can't run the nursery by herself."

He saw the shadow sweep over her features. "Lily told me what she said to you. I'm sorry. She's...feisty."

She shrugged. "She's protective."

"I'm her big brother. And practically twice her size."

"I never had any siblings, but I don't think size matters. You stick together. That's what family is for."

"It is. So...I'm staying."

She recoiled. "In Three Pines?"

"Mom can't afford to hire extra help while she heals, and Lily already works too hard. Noah can't leave his job, and Levi's got his hands full." He turned up his palms. "That leaves me, at least for a while."

Her shoulders sank. "You'll need the cottage, then."

Gamble had never thought you could actually watch dreams die, but grief was in her face. "I don't know."

"You'd stay at your mother's?"

"For now. When she's home...I'll have to see." He found himself driven to explain. "I haven't been inside the cottage yet."

She studied him silently, and he felt awkward and foolish. She was being nicer than he deserved.

He'd made her cry.

"Jezebel, it's— I—" He paused. "I was out of line when I said you weren't fit to wipe your shoes on her mat." He forced himself to meet her gaze. "You were right. Charlotte would have behaved better." Suddenly, he was weary to the bone. "I'm keeping you from your customers."

"True." She turned to go. Paused with one hand on the door. Faced him again, her shoulders stiff. "I probably can guess your answer, but I have to ask. If you find that you can't live there but aren't interested in selling, would you consider renting it to me?"

He flinched, but she rushed on before he could speak. "For Skeeter's sake. I'm aware that you don't want me there, but he isn't able to live alone, and he's a good man. He deserves to spend his declining years in someplace besides the nursing home. He's withering in that place, and I just can't stand by and let that happen." Her expression was all about challenge.

"I don't—"

Hurt vied with determination. "You don't have to answer now. Just think about it, okay?"

"Jezebel, don't take this the wrong way, but—"

"What else am I to understand? You don't consider me good enough to live in the house you built for the wife you still love. I don't claim to be a saint like her, but I'm not as bad as you make me out to be. There were two of us in that bed, Gamble Smith, and neither one of us had a gun to his head."

She stared at him. "You'd like me to tell you to forget it and just go away, but I can't do that. Skeeter is the closest thing to family I've had since I was five, and I'm not letting him down without fighting to the last second, even if you believe, as your sister obviously does, that I have no conscience."

She whirled away, then back. "She's right, you know, but not about seducing you. I felt sorry for you and wanted to help, long before I had any idea who you were. And maybe I was a little lonely myself.

What happened that night shouldn't have, but it did, and we just move on. But when it comes to that old man's life, you betcha I'll be a shark. I'll do whatever is necessary to keep him alive and as happy as I can possibly make him. If you aren't willing to help me, that's your privilege, even if it's wrong and selfish." Tears glittered in her eyes as she took the first step away from him.

In that moment, she was no longer only a siren, more than a bombshell whose allure he found tough to resist. Behind her outrageous beauty beat a heart that was passionate and courageous.

That generosity made her dangerous, but it also merited more respect than he'd given her. "Thank you."

She frowned. "For what?"

"Wishing to buy my mom flowers."

"Oh." Her vibrancy faded. "You're welcome." She opened the door.

"Jezebel."

She halted but remained facing away.

"I'll consider it," he said. "But I can't promise."

She nodded. "That's all I can ask." An awkward silence ensued. "Well...get a good night's sleep."

"Yeah." He pulled the keys from his pocket and began to walk to the car.

"Gamble?"

"Yeah?"

"You should consult your mom about your roses. I suspect they need pruning."

Then she was gone, leaving him shaking his head.

INSIDE, JEZEBEL plastered a big smile on her face for the benefit of Darrell and the rest of her protectors, as she made haste toward the ladies' room. So much of her clientele was male that it might as well have been her own private retreat, one more reliably sacrosanct than her office.

Once there, she locked the door and collapsed against it. Let her head fall back while panic reared and bucked like some half-wild stallion.

He was staying. Indefinitely.

Holy cow. How would she ever hide a pregnancy now?

You don't know, Jezebel. You can't be sure yet.

She had to leave. Run again. But where? Until Russ Bollinger was tried and convicted, she was at risk. But what about Skeeter?

Her thoughts staggered like a wino.

Okay. She made herself walk to the sink, splash some water on her face.

Maybe her inner certainty was just wishful thinking, the result of these months when she'd begun to settle in and send roots into the rich soil of Three Pines. The legacy of all the hours she'd spent dreaming about Gamble's cottage, the epitome of a life as opposite to the one she'd lived as she ever expected to see.

One more fantasy, this baby, one she'd cherished too long. She had no business trying to raise a child—what did she know about how a mother was supposed to act? Her memories of her own mother were rosy, yes, but was that reality or the blessing of time's patina?

She'd sure seen her share of bad mothers since.

Maybe she should go back to the cottage and assess it with critical eyes. Look for flaws instead of falling for the romance of it. Perhaps she could argue herself out of it. Find someplace else to go and take Skeeter with her.

And how, exactly, do you plan to support both of you?

She could still dance and make a good living.

But she didn't want to.

And if she was pregnant, that option was out anyway.

Okay. Okay. Calm down. Think clearly.

The facts were these: three more days until she could test. A trial scheduled soon, she hoped. She wouldn't show for some period after that, and by then, with luck Gamble might have returned to New York, and she'd be home free.

And if he doesn't?

"Shut up," she told the woman in the mirror. "I'm doing the best I can."

With a deep breath, she unlocked the door and steeled herself for a bravura performance as a woman with no worries.

CHAPTER NINE

LILY WAS UP and out the door at five-thirty, determined to visit with her mother before the myriad morning chores at the nursery began. If her mother was still asleep, she'd just sit with her, but she was willing to bet that Mama, even more of an early riser by nature, would be awake.

Others were stirring, she could see as she walked down the corridor to her mother's room. Very soon, the level of activity would be at full force, with breakfast and baths and doctors making rounds, but she had a sense of the world holding its breath just yet.

She didn't knock on her mother's partly opened door, just in case. Mama was still very weak and would sleep a great deal, the floor nurse assigned to her had said yesterday. Lily gave a gentle push and peeked inside.

Her mother's eyes opened. She smiled.

It was then that the sun rose for Lily. "Hi, Mama. Can you handle a visitor?"

"You bet." But her voice came out a croak, and when she tried to push herself higher on the pillow, she grimaced.

"Should you be moving?"

"I want to see you."

"I'm here." Lily adjusted the pillow behind her and stroked her hair. "How about some water?"

"Yes. Please." Her mother leaned forward and winced. Her hand shook on the cup, so Lily steadied it.

"Are you hurting, Mama?"

"I'm okay."

Lily could tell she wasn't. "Would you like me to find the nurse?"

"It's a half hour until I can take my next dose. Nothing for her to do."

"I can ask. I'll be right—" Half-turned, she stilled with the touch of her mother's hand on her arm.

"I'll make it. Sit and talk to me. That's the best medicine of all. Tell me how you're doing, sweetheart. Catch me up on everyone."

Lily pulled a chair close and sat clasping her mother's hand, careful not to jostle her IV. "I'm fine. Had to check on you before I started watering."

"I'm so sorry the burden of this has fallen most on you, honey."

"It's nothing, Mama. You're awake, and you're going to get well. That's all that matters."

"How's Cal doing?" her mother asked.

A picture of the thoroughly disreputable Calvin Robicheaux popped into her mind, his dark eyes gleaming with challenge. She shook her head to dislodge it.

"Is he helping you?"

Relief silenced her for a second. Mama hadn't read her mind, for a change. She was ready to talk business. "Depends on what you mean by *help*."

"She means am I lettin' you lie around like a pampered princess, sugar," a very familiar voice said from the doorway.

"Cal," her mother noted with obvious pleasure. "How nice."

"I have to keep tabs on my best girl," he said, approaching the bed. "You look a lot better awake, *chère*."

Lily leaped from her chair and gave him wide berth.

Smoothly, he replaced her and pressed a courtly kiss to her mother's hand, then frowned. "You're in pain, aren't you?"

His presumption galled Lily. "It's too soon for her next dose," she snapped.

"No? Well, let ol' Cal here see what he can manage. Don't go anywhere now, you hear?" He winked at her mother and left the room.

Her mother chuckled. "If I were thirty years younger…"

"You'd have better taste than that…that—"

"That what, honey? Scoundrel? Scamp? Oh, darling, I hope not. A man like that was born to make women's hearts beat fast."

"*Women* being the operative word. That alley cat wouldn't recognize monogamy if it bit him on the—"

"My, my, our Cal can rile you up, can't he?"

"He's obnoxious and rude and high-handed and—" Lily spluttered.

"And loyal and kind and brave," her mother noted. "And I'd bet that he's put in a lot of hours since I've been in here, hasn't he?"

"He's not kind," Lily said. "And I don't get what's so brave. He's an ex-con, Mama."

"Who made a dumb kid's mistake and paid for it," her mother admonished. "He's been honest and dependable ever since he's been with us, and he's put in hours he didn't get paid for, just because he believes in doing a job right. I'm surprised at you, Lily. You have a quick temper, but you're not usually unfair."

"Me? I'm not unfair—"

"Then why does he get under your skin so?" Her mother's eyes crinkled. "As if I couldn't guess."

"You don't know everything, Mama."

"Don' sass your mama, *chère*." Cal strolled in as though he had nothing better to do. He winked at

Lily, who scowled back at him. Then he stepped aside as the nurse entered.

"Mr. Robicheaux—"

"Oh, Cal, sugar, please."

The nurse dimpled. "Cal, then. Mrs. Smith, Cal says your medication isn't keeping up with your pain level. We can talk to the doctor about putting you on a demand system through your IV so you can have more control over your remediation."

"I don't like drugging myself. I'll do fine."

"Marian, *chère,* pain is hard on the body when it's trying to heal. You should take the offer, so you can be back with us sooner."

"My head gets fuzzy. I don't want to slip back—"

Lily's throat tightened. Her mother was afraid of falling back into unconsciousness. "That won't happen, will it?" she asked the nurse.

"No. And we won't let you sleep too much, but at the moment, rest is critical. Don't worry, though— later today, the physical therapist will be here, and he'll be putting you to work."

"That's good. I need to get out of this place. I want to go home. Tend to my plants."

Lily heard the longing in her mother's voice, and tears threatened. There was nothing she desired more than to have her mother home, too. "You will, Mama. But you have to rest first. You take your medication, and I'll get on to work, so you don't have to be concerned. The plants are in good hands."

"Of course they are, sweetheart." She accepted Lily's hug, then glanced past her. "And I thank you for standing by my daughter, Cal. She's lucky to have you."

Cal glanced at Lily with a slow, wicked smile, then turned it into another, sweeter one for her mother. "She thinks so, too, *chère*. She's just shy about sayin' it."

Her mother giggled. *Giggled*.

Lily glared at Cal and crossed the room. "'Bye, Mama. I'll see you this evening. I love you."

"I love you, too, sweet girl."

Lily charged down the hall.

"You are, you know, sugar. Lucky to have me." Cal caught up with her with no seeming effort.

"Bite me, Calvin."

He held his gimme cap over his heart. "Oh, darlin', I thought you'd never ask."

She broke into a trot, but his chuckles followed her.

GAMBLE LEFT THE NURSERY after a grinning Cal and a disgruntled Lily arrived. He'd already done the morning watering, just as Lily had shown him the day before; now it was his turn to visit his mom.

But he wasn't going to face her and be forced to admit that he hadn't yet gone inside the cottage. Not because she would look down on him for the lack, but because she'd fretted over him so when he was lost in grief; he had no wish to give her reason to worry over him ever again.

However much he dreaded confronting the ruins of a dream, it was time. And despite Jezebel's offer, he must do it alone. He entered the lane marked by the sign Charlotte had designed and he had painted. His heartbeat picked up as the truck rolled into the tunnel of trees dotted, here and there, by delicate dogwood blossoms, small, creamy stars in cool, dense shade.

When he emerged into stark sunlight, he blinked against the glare.

In the sprawling green glade, the noose of memory waited for him.

He stopped the pickup just before the final bend. Breathed deep. Approached the gate.

Welcome To Honey Creek Cottage. Faded but still there in her flowing script.

He got out, opened it, brushed one hand over the words.

Then jumped back in, gunned the engine and shot down the gravel drive. Didn't allow himself to pause until he'd come to a halt in front of the garage that had once been his studio. Maybe going in the back door would be easier.

As he climbed the two steps and dug for the key that had never left his key ring, his gaze arrested on the trellis and its rambler rose. Charlotte had hoped for the scent to waft into the kitchen, and it had. Likewise, the honeysuckle planted outside their bedroom window had perfumed many a night and greeted them each morning.

The canes of the damask rose tangled together, some of them rubbing others raw. Jezebel was right. They needed pruning.

As he pulled open the screen door, he noted the worn paint beside the handle where time and hands had eroded the color.

Sweetheart Blue. He could still recall the day he'd finished the last coat and hung the door, twelve, no, thirteen years before. When they'd been young, and life had been so full of promise.

He unlocked the door and stepped inside the mudroom that led to the kitchen, glancing around. His mother's old washer and dryer, which she'd given them until they could afford better. Instead, they'd paid medical bills and he'd learned to replace belts and motors.

Get on with it. At this rate, Mom will be out of the hospital before you finish the tour.

So, steeling himself, he walked into Charlotte's kitchen.

The first thing he noticed was the absence of mouthwatering aromas. Even after she'd died, they'd lingered. She had been one hell of a cook, and old-fashioned about it, to boot. She'd refused to let him begin his day with anything less than a full breakfast, no matter how often that had meant her dragging herself from bed and much-needed rest.

And he'd let her, once he'd understood what it meant to her not to be an invalid.

His veins might be clogged from the bacon and butter-drenched biscuits, the fluffy, golden eggs, the strong, just-right coffee…but he hadn't cared then and still couldn't. Man, had those meals been delicious. Pot roast tender enough to cut with a fork, pies with light, flaky crusts…never before or since had he eaten so well.

For a moment, the room took on the glow it had once possessed, and he could almost see her there at the stove, humming to herself, blond tendrils escaping from the ponytail and, heat-curled, trailing over her nape. He'd cross the room as quietly as possible and attempt to kiss that spot before she heard him—

And the smile, her smile when she turned…the one reserved solely for him.

The image dissolved then, and the old, dark guilt struck. He gripped the counter's edge and suffered, once again, the raking claws of loss.

But to his surprise, he also felt the faint, soft touch of that long-treasured pleasure, as if something of Charlotte hovered nearby.

He paused, closed his eyes. Listened for all he was worth.

Please, he said to her in silence. Be here. *Know how much I wish—*

Too much. More than was possible. Certainly more than he deserved.

Any sense of her vanished. He swallowed hard and pushed forward into the rest of the house.

In the living room, he was confronted with the only one of his paintings to survive the night he'd tried to paint Charlotte to keep from losing her completely—and, consumed by rage at his inability to do so, had snapped stretcher bars like matchsticks, sliced canvases to ragged strips. Grief had howled in his ears, and he'd been reaching for the one she'd loved most: the cottage as they'd dreamed it before it was built.

Every slashing tear would have hurt her, but none more than that one. A remnant of sanity had stilled his hand. He'd fallen to the floor, clutching it, and the next morning, his mother had found him there. Levi had been summoned to spirit him away, and during his absence, his mother and Lily had cleaned up the wreckage. Dismantled, too, the nursery he'd made his mother leave alone as his penance.

Thank God that room was empty now. He had no idea what had happened to any of it, even the crib he'd poured so many hours into making.

And he didn't care.

He halted for a moment in front of the fireplace and studied the only remaining sample of his previous work.

Realized he was better now. Painted with a surer hand.

But one more calculated. This piece still vibrated with youth and hope. Sorrow had been a stranger to him then, as had remorse. The young man—boy, really—who'd created this had imagined no sins past forgiveness.

Gamble turned away from the reminder of the best part of him. Reluctantly, he made his way to the second heart of this place: the bedroom. The bed where the child who killed Charlotte had been created.

Each step dragged at him, drained him. If he'd ever considered living here again, the notion died now. Being inside these walls was sheer torture, where once he'd felt embraced. Safe and cherished. Strong.

Desperate for distraction as he moved down the hall, he yanked his attention from the past to the present and noticed the lack of cobwebs or dust.

His mother's doing, almost certainly, in hope that he would change his mind and return for her birthday. Never thinking that she might wind up fighting for her life.

Suddenly, he yearned to be done with this and nearly wheeled to escape and head for the hospital. Surely he'd faced enough demons.

And let them better you, if you can't open that last door.

He clasped the knob and shoved. Forced himself inside.

Sunlight poured through sparkling beveled-glass windows, casting rainbows on the honey-gold pine floors. How many hours had he spent, measuring, cutting, fitting boards…varnishing them to a satin glow? Laughing and talking with Charlotte, who plied him with endless glasses of sweet tea.

The bed was still theirs, but her serene cream and blue linens were gone. In their place was a comforter in forest green, ocean-deep blue, merlot-rich burgundy and coppery bronze. No more frilly curtains, no crystal decanters. He strode to the closet and hesitated, uncertain what he wished to see, her clothes or their absence.

He pulled the door open, and emptiness mocked him.

Mom, why—?

But he knew. He'd roared at her when she'd suggested going through Charlotte's things, giving them away. Ordered her out of his house.

She'd kept coming back, but the subject was not reopened. Her determination to have him back into life, however, had not abated.

She wanted him to face this, but she had tried to block the worst of the blows.

He glanced past his own clothes, spread to take up more of the space, sniffing for any trace of Charlotte that might have lingered.

All he could smell, though, was cedar.

And he couldn't hear her voice in his head anymore. Panic jittered inside him as he tore through memory, grasping for any snippet.

Mom, how could you do this? You've stolen her from me. I've lost her. He charged from the room, head swiveling from side to side as he sought evidence of his wife's existence and realized that, save for memory, she'd been expunged, every last whisper of her, from the place that was, ever and always, hers. Only hers.

He slammed outside, already yanking the keys from his pocket, leaped into the truck and shifted it into Reverse. He backed from the drive so fast he narrowly missed one of Charlotte's prized dogwoods—

He jammed on the brakes, threw the vehicle into Park—

Grasped the steering wheel until his knuckles turned white—

Then dropped his head onto crossed arms.

JEZEBEL DROVE down the lane, intending to study the cottage in solitude and hoping to find that it had lost its hold on her. That she could let her dream go.

Distracted by her thoughts, she nearly ran into the back of a pickup, a figure crumpled in the driver's seat. She braked to a halt and leaped out, leaving her door open.

She neared and recognized him.

Gamble. Oh, dear heaven. Was he—

She was almost close enough to grab for the door handle when she realized that his shoulders were shaking. She backed away from a moment too private to be shared with a stranger.

But before she could, he lifted his head and spotted her.

Jezebel froze. He looked awful. Ravaged. Wounded, soul-deep. "I—I'm sorry. I was just—" She tensed, expecting him to erupt from the truck and let her have it, full-bore.

He merely stared as if too exhausted to react. What to say? If she'd ever felt more awkward in her life, she couldn't recall it.

He seemed so lost, she couldn't allow herself to yield to the urge to flee. Instead, she tackled the situation head-on. "Are you coming or leaving?"

He didn't answer, but a muscle in his jaw jumped.

She inhaled a deep breath and soldiered on. "Would you like some company?"

He flinched. Though she would rather run, she made herself take a step closer. "Gamble, I'll turn around and drive out now, if that's what you prefer, but if you'd rather not be alone—"

"Stop talking," he barked. He jerked the door open and charged out, clutching the frame. His eyes were burning holes. "Why are you—" With visible effort, he halted. Focused on the ground. "It doesn't matter why you're here. Just go, Jezebel." A shudder racked him. "Please."

No option seemed more attractive than doing as he asked, but an inner voice whispered that even if she were the worst choice, he needed someone right now.

But he was also a man who bottled things inside. He wouldn't be comfortable talking this out; few men were, and he was more contained than most.

So she'd distract him. She squared her shoulders and strolled past him. "I've been reading up on azaleas, but there's one thing I can't figure. How can you be sure when you're overfertilizing?"

The silence was deafening, but she didn't look back. A convict tiptoeing past the guards couldn't be more nervous, but she figured one of two things would happen: he'd explode or he'd answer her. Either reaction would get him out of the obviously very bad place he was in. She wasn't afraid that he'd hurt her physically; for all the complications of their brief liaison, she'd witnessed a gentleness and concern in him that relieved her of that worry.

She forged on, approaching the nearest tree. "This is a dogwood, right? It's a pity they can't bloom longer, but I guess we wouldn't appreciate them as much if they did." *Chattering your way to the firing line, huh, Jez?*

"Do you have to prune these, too? And is it important to seal the wounds?"

"Jezebel." His voice was flat.

"Yes?"

"What the hell are you doing?" She caught a faint note of curiosity.

She smiled weakly, as only someone stalling the executioner could. "Admiring your yard?"

He exhaled in a gust. "What would I have to say to get you to go away?"

She gnawed her lip, then met his gaze honestly. "I'm not sure."

His shoulders relaxed just a bit. He seemed to be weighing and discarding a series of answers. "I thought we agreed that I'd think about renting the place to you. That involves waiting. You. Wait. I...think."

"I got that, but—" She tilted her head in acknowledgment. "I was trying to do you a favor and talk myself out of it."

"You were, huh?" With every exchange, she could see the despair in him lifting.

"And did it work?" he asked.

She shook her head. "Sorry. I still love it." He visibly withdrew; she hastened to reassure him. "It's okay, Gamble. I know you don't want me here, and I totally understand why you'd keep this beautiful place to yourself. Anyway, it's not as if this is the first time I've ever been denied something I wished for. Just part of life. So if you'd see fit to let me walk around it one more time, I promise I won't ever bother you—"

He held up a hand. She ceased her chatter. Watched him engage in an inner debate.

Finally, he shut the truck door. "Would you like to go inside?"

Her heart did a quick tumble. She bit her lip. "No."

He frowned. "No?"

"Oh, of course I do. More than anything. But it wouldn't be fair."

"To whom?"

She met his gaze. "Either of us. I have no desire to be taunted with what I can't have, and you don't want me trespassing in your special place." She shrugged. "I don't blame you, Gamble, honestly I don't. If I'd ever loved anyone like you loved her, I'd be tempted to keep this cottage a shrine forever."

"But you wouldn't."

"How can you be sure?"

"You'd open it up as a home for wayward girls and lost old men and stray puppies. Even if you couldn't live there, you'd find a way to share it with the downtrodden."

She regarded him with caution. "I don't need anyone's pity, if that's the reason you're offering."

His glance was a laser slice of warning. "Neither do I." He started toward the house. "Last chance, Jezebel. Come along or forget it."

She hesitated, torn between longing and warning.

He paused at the front door and held it open, his stance challenging.

"Why are you doing this, Gamble?"

As she approached, she noted that his eyes were bleak. "Beats the hell out of me." He gestured her to precede him.

Jezebel took the first step and prayed for disappointment.

CHAPTER TEN

WHEN SHE GOT INSIDE, however, Jezebel was alone. She started to turn and ask him why, but realized she could not.

She and Gamble had been physically as close as two people ever could—but they were strangers, for all that. Some questions were too intimate for even friends to ask. She'd bluffed her way this far, but her nerve wasn't sufficient to dare more.

And, truth be told, she was relieved to be able to explore this house alone.

Then her heart sank. From the first glance, she understood that no matter how much time he granted her, she would wish for more.

This was it…the house of her dreams.

As she wandered from room to room, she found herself torn between laughing and crying. You could literally feel the devotion that bolstered every board, exuded from each stroke of paint. The imprint of grief lingered, yes, but she was wrapped, above all, in a silken cocoon of tenderness and warmth and… there was only the one word for it: love. Of a kind she'd only ever imagined.

She chided herself not to tarry, but she would have gladly stayed forever if she hadn't known that outside waited a man for whom every second she forced him to remain was torment.

By the time she walked back onto the front porch, she was in tears. Desperately, she sought to stem them.

"Don't." Misery knotted with anger.

She started to speak. Couldn't. Ducked her head and hurried past him to her car.

Just before she reached it, heavy footsteps thundered behind her. He grabbed her arm. "Where are you going?"

She didn't try to escape him but didn't look at him, either.

"Damn it, why are you crying? Better not be for me."

At that, she whirled. "A stone would weep in that place."

He reared back as if stung. "What's wrong with it? Not good enough for you after all?"

"No." She sniffed. Brushed at her eyes. "I'd sell my soul to live there. I'd do nearly anything to give Skeeter that chance, but—"

"But what?"

She met his gaze. "It's beautiful, Gamble. More

than. I almost wish you hadn't let me go inside." She lifted her palms. "But I wouldn't have missed it for anything. It's every dream I never dared to have."

"And?"

"No one deserves that place but you. I can feel you, both of you, in every room. How you must have loved her." Tears spurted again. "And how obviously she felt cherished by you."

He recoiled as if she'd struck him. "You don't know what you're talking about."

"I understand how painful it must be to be without her—"

"You understand nothing." Bone-deep sorrow reverberated in his voice. To remain in Three Pines must be hellish, all the more so because he couldn't be sure how long he must stay.

"So tell me," she said.

He stilled. Peered out for only an instant from the fortress he'd built around him, before retreating again. "No," he said quietly. "That's a story I will tell only once, to one woman."

"All right." Clearly, she wasn't that special person. The anguish in his gaze kept the worst of her hurt at bay. "But the invitation's open."

"I'm not one of your charity cases."

"No. You're not. And I can't give you what you want most, but there's something I can do, if you'll let me. I make a good friend, Gamble." She extended her hand. "Goodbye. Thank you for letting me inside. I can only imagine how hard that was for you to do."

For a minute, she thought he was going to refuse the gesture. At last, his hand rose to clasp hers.

And despite herself, she shivered at his touch. What a complex man he was, strong and yet so vulnerable, obviously capable of great love and dying without it. Unable to bend enough to ask for help.

And a brilliant painter, from the one example she'd seen above the fireplace.

That he might also be the father of a child even now growing inside her body was a complication she couldn't contemplate right now. No matter how desperately she wished to be a mother, Gamble would be better off if she was mistaken. He had too much to deal with already.

"So," she said, withdrawing her hand. "See you around, I guess."

He watched her but didn't speak.

She got in her car and slowly drove away.

GAMBLE LISTENED to the engine in the wreck of a car that was running rough as she departed. He flexed the fingers of the hand she'd clasped, and quickly shut them.

I make a good friend.

She was a hell of a lover, too.

But neither mattered.

Or mattered too much.

Who was the last friend he'd had, besides his family? He couldn't recall. Charlotte had been his closest companion since they were kids. His brothers had filled any need for male company. In New York, he'd kept to himself, mostly. He was there to work. To discover if he could create a life worth living without—

Enough.

This time, he realized with a shock, the voice was not his mother's or Charlotte's.

The voice of reason…was his.

Reluctantly, he faced the cottage. For the first time, the figure on the porch was not Charlotte.

It was, damn her hide, Jezebel Hart. Face glowing, tears and wonder shining in her eyes.

"No—" he groaned. Squeezed his lids shut. Shook his head to dislodge her.

It's every dream I never dared have.

"No!" he shouted. "It's not your dream. It's Charlotte's. It's—" *Mine.*

Mine.

He opened his eyes again, his chest too tight to breathe. And viewed the cottage, just for an instant, through Jezebel's eyes.

Not scarred with agony, not tarnished by guilt but

freed from either, a sturdy and graceful haven once blessed by laughter.

And sanctified by love.

No one deserves that place but you.

"You're wrong, Jezebel. No one has earned it less," he murmured, but within him, shame stirred. He had buried the best of him here and turned a place of beauty into a crypt. As with the fairy tale, the brambles were beginning to creep in and would soon bury it alive.

He was lauded for his ability to render beauty with a brush, to transform women into enchantresses, yet his single finest creation was dying before his eyes.

For the sake of the love that once lived here, it was time to bring the cottage back to life.

JEZEBEL WAS GRATEFUL they were so busy tonight; it left her little time to think. To grieve over the loss of the cottage.

To worry about what to do for Skeeter.

"Jezebel, we need an impartial judge over here," Chappy hollered from the far end of the bar.

"For what?" She juggled a full tray, served a round and cleared the table of the last. Her feet hurt, her back ached and her left elbow felt the strain of the load.

"Me and Larry think a man will be quicker to get cut off if he forgets Valentine's Day than a woman's birthday. Zell and Louie here say just the opposite, but neither one of them has been within a country mile of a woman's bed since God was a pup."

"I've been married for forty-seven years," Zell reminded them.

"My point exactly." Chappy grinned.

"And you've been married, what is it, three times?" Louie asked.

"Got more experience, don't I?" Chappy asked. "Been with more women."

"Rejected by more, that's for sure," Louie said. "Definitely been cut off more often."

"Heard tell Clarissa had in mind to cut something else off besides bed sport, something real personal," Larry added.

"Damn."

"Hell."

All of them winced.

"Get the jar, Darrell," Jezebel said.

"Now, Jezebel, a man can't be held accountable for swearing when his privates are threatened."

"We're all accountable, on earth or in the hereafter. Pay up."

"Harpy," Louie muttered. "St. Peter will be a breeze after you."

"Oh, sweetie." She pressed a kiss to his cheek. "How you do flatter."

Laughter echoed around the room.

She heard the door open and prepared to greet the new arrival.

Levi Smith smiled at her. She smiled back.

Until Gamble came in right behind him.

The woman in her had to simply pause and appreciate the sight of the brothers Smith. A girl's heart could stop cold at the sheer amount of maleness entering the premises.

Gamble was scanning the room, so she had a second to compose herself.

A second wasn't long enough.

When his eyes locked on hers, she realized that she was the object of his search. For one unguarded instant, it was obvious that he was uneasy about how she'd treat him, what she might reveal by her reaction after the soul-baring experience of the morning. Time slowed. She was a moth trapped inside a bell jar, sealed off from the world.

Then it hit her that the entire room had grown quiet. And a scowling Darrell was rounding the bar toward Gamble.

She burst the crystal prison. "Levi, how are you? Gamble." She nodded, her smile fast and brilliant. "How's your mom this evening?"

"A little better, I think," Levi answered, glancing between Darrell and Gamble with questions in his expression.

Gamble said nothing, but he wasn't shying from the mountain of man headed his way.

"Here's a booth." She hastened to clear it. "Have a seat, and I'll take your order."

"A beer for me," Levi said, but made no move to sit, obviously ready to defend his brother.

Still Gamble remained silent.

"Darrell, can I see you for a minute?"

When he didn't reply, she sighed. "Men." She stepped in front of him. "Levi will have a beer, Darrell. What would you like, Gamble?" she asked over her shoulder.

"A piece of Darrell is fine."

She wheeled on him. "Sit. Both of you." To Darrell, she pointed to the bar. "You. Back to work."

All three of them might as well have been deaf. Around them a buzz arose.

So she dropped a glass on the floor. The crash startled everyone. "What the hell," Darrell yelped.

"Now that I have everyone's attention." She kept her tone saccharine sweet. "Chappy, will you please open the door and fan it? We seem to have an epidemic of testosterone poisoning. Louie, you phone Shirley to pick up her husband, who appears to have the most serious case. Tell her not to bring the kids. It might be catching."

"That's just cold," Chappy said.

"No call to be insulting," Louie grumbled.

"When I start insulting, you'll know it. Now I'm going to get the broom. On the way back, I hope to find everyone enjoying themselves immensely." She gazed around the room. "Am I getting through?"

Many words were mumbled, but none was audible as first one man, then another, shuffled off to resume pool games and poker hands.

She heard a chuckle behind her and turned to note Levi grinning while a disgruntled Gamble dropped into one side of the booth. "Like a hand with that broom?" Levi asked.

"You—" she pointed "—might have potential."

"Sweetheart, you have no idea," said the reigning heartthrob of Three Pines.

Jezebel laughed.

"And you—" she spoke to Darrell "—owe the jar a dollar."

Darrell muttered and cast scathing glances at Gamble all the way back to the bar.

Before he could get a bill out of his wallet, however, she took one of her own and slipped it into the hole in the top. When he lifted his eyebrows, she explained. "Not fair to make you pay when I'm the one who dropped the glass and startled you." She touched his hand. "But I don't need protecting from Gamble."

"I'll still kick his ass if he hurts you."

He stuck in a dollar anyway, then walked off to draw Levi's beer.

Jezebel sighed and headed for the broom.

LEVI HUNG AROUND for two beers and a game of pool, then left, citing early surgery.

Gamble stayed behind and nursed his second beer. Around him, the tabletop was littered with napkins on which he'd sketched the denizens of this bar.

Louie arguing with Chappy.

Darrell polishing a glass, eyes cocked to the side to glare warning at Gamble.

Jezebel bent over, wiping a table.

With a loaded tray, laughing.

Jezebel again, leaning against the bar, arms outstretched in lazy welcome, her braid unwound, waves of black hair cascading over—

"Surely that beer could stand to be replaced," she said.

He shoved that napkin beneath the others. Scrambled to stack all of them, but the flimsy papers scattered, some floating to the floor.

"I'll get it—"

"Don't—"

They crouched down at the same time and knocked heads.

"Ow." She emerged with a fistful of napkins in one

hand, rubbing her forehead with the other. "You okay?" She gave a nervous laugh.

"Yeah. Let me have those."

"No sweat. I get paid to clean. Well, not exactly paid, but…" Her voice died off as she spotted the remaining drawings. "What's this?" Delight bubbled. "Look at Louie. That's exactly him. And Chappy." She glanced down at the ones clutched in her hands. "Oh. Oh, I'm so sorry. Here—" She laid them on the table and began to smooth them.

Gamble slapped his hand on top of them.

But it was too late. She studied this batch in total silence. There was no way she could miss that the vast majority were of her.

Including the one, just out of his reach, where she wore nothing he'd ever seen her in. The filmy gown, draping off one shoulder, emerald green in his mind, to bring out her eyes. A barefoot Gypsy, a barbarian's plunder of bronze jewelry at throat and ears, her generous mouth an unpainted rose. A hint of nipples and dark triangle beneath the fabric clinging to her Junoesque curves. Yet for all the drawing's eroticism, it was, at heart, romantic.

"I seem…soft," she said. "But I'm not. I can't afford to be," she murmured. "You've made me beautiful."

Finally, he spoke. "You are."

"No. Sure, I've got—" She gestured dismissal at

her curves. "This. I can't complain—it's provided me work when I didn't have the education to be more, but men always assume—" She broke off, her cheeks stained a hectic red. "I'll get you that beer." Reluctantly, she relinquished her hold on the napkin but trailed her fingers over it before she stepped back.

"Would you like to have it?" He surprised himself by asking. "Take them all." Even though he'd like to keep that one himself. "I can always draw more."

"My own Gamble Smith collection? People pay you for your work."

He smiled, touched by her hesitation. "It's hardly polished. And I'm not famous."

"You will be, if these and the painting I saw today are any indication." She stiffened. "I'm sorry. I shouldn't have brought that up."

He was surprised that her mention only engendered a small ache. "I'm, uh, going to begin cleaning the grounds of the cottage tomorrow afternoon when I finish helping Lily and visit Mom."

A long, awkward pause ensued.

"I'm still not sure, Jezebel. What to do with the place, I mean." He exhaled. "I'm sorry. That doesn't help you."

"It's okay. I…understand. I'll manage."

He was certain she would, but that wasn't the point.

"I should get your beer."

"No." He grasped her arm, and both of them froze. "I have to go. Nursery work starts with the sun."

"Oh. Of course." Her fingers hovered above the napkins she'd carefully stacked.

"They're yours." He rose. Stood beside her. Smelled her hair, just a whiff of spice and roses past the smoke and beer scents in the air.

A quiver threaded through her frame. She lifted her gaze to his. "I— Thank you." She gathered them up carefully. "I can't imagine what that would be like," she said as she pressed them gently between her palms. "To have such an amazing talent. You take my breath away," she said as she turned toward the bar.

That makes two of us.

When she was almost out of hearing, he stirred himself to speak. "If you—" He cleared his throat. "If you'd care to drop by tomorrow and—" He lifted his palms. "I don't know, supervise or something—"

"I…" Her smile was hesitant, but even that much eased something inside him. "I might."

He watched her go and had the thought that he'd been sketching her all evening, but he still hadn't managed to capture the mystery that was Jezebel Hart.

But a part of him wanted it.

Too damn much.

CHAPTER ELEVEN

JEZEBEL'S PHONE rang the next morning. "Hello?"

"Ms. Hart, this is assistant D.A. Gary Lansing."

Her stomach clenched. "Yes?"

"We have a trial date in the Bollinger case."

"When?" She should be happy to get it over with, but she wasn't ready to face Vegas again.

"Jury selection begins Monday."

"What will that mean for me?"

"Forming a jury shouldn't require but a few days at most. We'd like you to go ahead and travel to Vegas right away."

Dread crawled up her spine; she wished to be done with Vegas and her life there. "I really can't be gone for more than the absolute minimum time required for my testimony, Mr. Lansing. I have a business to run." *And even if I didn't, I have no desire to be anywhere near Russ Bollinger or his goons.*

"Our office can't afford last-minute tickets, Ms. Hart. Can't you find someone to take over for you?"

Darrell could handle things if necessary; that wasn't the point. "Not really."

"I see." His voice said otherwise.

If only she could afford to pay her own way.

If only she didn't have to go.

"Mr. Lansing, are you certain my testimony is crucial?"

"Ms. Hart, we can compel you to show up."

If Gamble accepted her purchase offer on the cottage, she couldn't spare the funds for a full-fare ticket, but she longed to be done with her past.

"I'll manage, Mr. Lansing. Just let me know when I have to be there." She steadied her voice with effort. "You can count on me."

"You'd be safer in our protection, Ms. Hart."

She was skeptical. Russ Bollinger was no one to fool with. Still, he had no idea where she was. "I'll be fine."

"Stay available, Ms. Hart." The threat was clear.

"I'll do my duty, Mr. Lansing." No matter how much she didn't like it.

"Very well. I'll talk to you soon."

Jezebel dropped the phone into the cradle and rubbed that hand on her jeans as if to scrub off the taint of her past.

GAMBLE PAUSED at the back door of the cottage and steeled himself, then stepped inside and crossed the kitchen to place the soft drinks inside the refrigerator. Checked to see if he should make ice, but the trays were full. He cracked two open and dumped them into the bin, then refilled them. Tried not to remember that he'd promised Charlotte an icemaker one day, but that day—that money—had never materialized.

He forced the thought away and focused on the hours ahead of him. He wasn't sure if the utilities had remained on or someone in his family had had them reinstated, but he was grateful. Spring in East Texas wasn't gentle. A cold drink would be welcome before the afternoon was gone.

He wondered if Jezebel was a Coke or Pepsi girl. He'd bought both and felt like a thorough fool for doing it.

Gratefully, he escaped the house and made his way toward the shed of garden tools he assumed were still there. On the route past the garage, he glanced at the door and stutter-stepped just a little. He hadn't entered his studio yet. He wasn't ready.

But he remembered the feel of the pencil in his hand, sketching last night, and knew that for a lie. An urge to hold a brush, to mix pigment and oil, was rising within him. Emerald-green and tumbling black curls. Bronze against the white velvet of her skin—

He recoiled from the doorknob as if an electrical shock had passed through him. He could not paint Jezebel in this place so intimately entwined with Charlotte.

Not until he fulfilled his promise to the woman he'd loved more than life.

And he was nowhere near up for that.

He stalked to the shed and grabbed as many tools as he could carry.

And walked around the other side of the house to begin.

JEZEBEL DROVE TOWARD the cottage, reminding herself not to get her hopes up just because he'd invited her. She was dressed to help, not supervise; another set of hands would mean he'd finish that much sooner. If being in this place was so hard for him, then she would do her best to speed his progress. She'd gone one step further and made food, almost like a picnic, though calling it one seemed inappropriate.

Things had eased between them last night, but he was obviously still suffering.

Did you understand, Charlotte Smith, what you had? She sighed and rested her head on one hand. Since she was orphaned, no one had felt a tenth of that for her; doubtful anyone ever would.

But there were times you just had to stand back and admire something beautiful, like a perfect rose or a glorious sunset—or a perfect love—and appreciate it without trying to make it yours. Or wishing for more than the simple pleasure of that moment. The knowledge that such miracles existed.

Miracles, though, carried a cost. From the stories she'd heard and from observing his reactions, Gamble Smith had given himself to his wife so completely that when he lost her, he lost himself. She'd never experienced such suffering; the thought of a bond that strong both compelled and terrified her.

The turnoff appeared ahead. She straightened and made it, resolutely ignoring the other thread running through her mind: those drawings, one in particular, and the hours of the night she'd spent poring over them, sifting for meaning as a treasure hunter combs beach sand.

Nonsense. He's an artist. He draws because it's what he does.

But so many. Of her. And the invitation to come here…

Don't read anything into it, Jez. Two more days and both your worlds could be blown to smithereens if that test is positive.

That was the cold blast of water that could rid her of any illusions about sketches or filmy dresses or men who were entombed in a castle of grief.

She nearly turned around then, before he could spot her driving up.

Then, she realized, it was too late. He stood not ten yards away, sweaty and so gorgeous your tongue could fall out of your mouth, clearing tangled vines from the fence.

And clearly no more sure of himself than she was, based on the discomfort on his face.

She drew a deep breath for courage and emerged. "Hi."

He was silent, his gaze troubled.

She was off-stride herself, no idea what to say to him, how to act. If she should stay or go.

Her history said, *flee. Forget this place, this man and all his troubles. His too-potent magnetism.*

But she was a woman of her word; she'd offered to help, and help she would. "I, uh, I'll just put this on the porch." She took one step, then another until she squeezed past him through the narrow gate opening, cooler in hand.

She'd never finished high school, but she read voraciously. Somewhere she'd learned about pheromones and their deadly allure. The way two people could be drawn into each other's orbit because chemically they clicked, beyond the bounds of logic or propriety or sense.

Maybe Gamble's receptors weren't operational.

Unfortunately, hers were on overload.

Hot, sweaty, gorgeous. Talented. Lonely. Strong,

yet made vulnerable by an ability to love that staggered her…Gamble Smith packed quite a punch, like it or not.

Then his gaze rose to hers, a hot flame of blue, quickly smothered.

But not before her stomach fluttered in response.

"You came." His voice, in contrast, was leaden.

"You invited me." Her jaw stiffened. "I'm here to help, but if you'd rather I go, I'll just leave this food."

"You cooked for me?"

She already felt enough the idiot. "You don't eat?"

Behind her, silence. She clenched her fingers on the handle of the cooler.

Then he chuckled. Faint, rusty, yes…but she'd heard it.

When she faced him, chagrin not derision greeted her.

He rubbed one hand on the back of his neck. "I wouldn't blame you," he said, nodding toward her white-knuckled grip. "Look—I'm not much good with women." He shook his head. "Not that great with people in general."

"Huh. Coulda fooled me."

His head jerked up, a retort forming.

She found a smile.

His answering one was rueful. "My brothers got all the charm in the family. Lily's a spitfire, and I always had…never mind."

Not hard to complete his sentence. "Charlotte must have been amazing."

"She was." Those gorgeous eyes sharpened on her. "I'm supposed to get over her. Put her behind me."

"You will when you're ready."

He stiffened. "I'll never forget her."

"I didn't say you should. I'd like to think that if anyone ever loved me that way, he'd always keep a part of me within him."

"I don't have the right," she thought he murmured, gazing off into the distance.

"Why not?"

He didn't answer, his concentration elsewhere.

Jezebel pressed her lips together and waited. The day's heat bore down; her shirt stuck to her back. In the still air, she heard the buzzing of bees, a bird's warble. She closed her eyes and found herself, for once, caught in a moment where she could simply…breathe. Despite the presence of a man she found both attractive and maddening, beyond the grasp of all her worries, Jezebel felt an overwhelming sense of peace.

"She used to say that this was as close to heaven as she could imagine."

Jezebel's eyes popped open, to see his unguarded. "It's incredibly beautiful. How did you find it?"

"My folks hoped to build a house here one day, but Dad died before they got the chance. My mom couldn't keep up the payments with four kids to raise, so she had to sell. It came on the market when I was in college, waiting for Charlotte to graduate high school. I already knew I wasn't going to finish. I went away the first year as part of a bargain I made with Mom. She said that if what Charlotte and I had was the real thing, it would survive my absence."

"Obviously, it did."

He smiled ruefully. "*Absence* is too strong a word. I was home every weekend, and we were on the phone each night we were apart."

Jezebel laughed.

"Anyway, I decided when this place became available that I had a better use for the money I'd saved for college. I offered it as a down payment for Mom first, since it had been her and Dad's dream, but she said she couldn't bear to leave the last place she'd lived in with him."

"Your family is so amazing." Jezebel didn't even attempt to keep the envy from her voice. "I would have given anything for that kind of devotion."

"Where's your family?"

"I don't have one." She jutted her jaw, daring him to delve deeper.

"I'm sorry hear that." His eyebrows rose, and he surprised her. "But I think you're wrong."

"What do you mean?"

"You're as devoted to Skeeter as any granddaughter could be. Darrell has appointed himself your big brother." His grin was rueful. "I can't decide if Louie and Chappy are the crazy uncles most people hide in the closet or a couple of overage bickering siblings."

She had to laugh, even as she marveled at how right he was. And unbent a little. "I grew up in foster homes, and I always swore that one day I'd have a real house, with a white picket fence and babies and puppies and kittens."

He grimaced. "And I'm standing in the way of that."

"It's okay, Gamble." She clasped his arm, and felt a visceral thrill. Quickly, she withdrew. "I can't imagine how I'd react, in your shoes."

He stared at her for a moment in which she had the sense that he'd experienced the shock, too. His gaze honed in on her with a flicker of hunger. One hand lifted as if he might touch her, and longing rose within her for him to do exactly that. *Touch me, Gamble. Let me touch you.*

She closed her eyes against the temptation, and as soft as the caress of a summer morning breeze, his fingers brushed her hair. Trailed down the braid from which curls were already escaping. Drifted over the swell of her breast and electrified her every nerve ending. A small sigh escaped her.

The contact abruptly ceased. She braved a

glimpse of his features, though she wasn't sure she wanted to know.

Heat, fading rapidly into confusion. Tumult.

He stepped away. "I have work to do."

It isn't wrong for you to live, she yearned to tell him, but didn't. He was like an animal that had been whipped, too spooked for easy trust.

So she put the cooler down. "I have gloves in the car," she said as neutrally as she could manage. "Shall I begin on the roses? I read up on pruning them last night. It's nearly too late, but it can still be done."

"Why would you—" He clamped his mouth shut.

"The sooner you're finished, the quicker you can leave Three Pines," she reminded him. "And I'm not assuming anything about what will happen then."

"I don't understand you." He didn't wait for an explanation, though, and started down the steps.

Me, either, she thought.

HER HAIR WAS THICK and silken, a mass of waves straining to break from their bonds. Gamble clenched his hand against the feel of it, so alive and beckoning. *Set me loose. Free me.*

The call was repeated inside his chest, echoed in his head, a lure he had to ignore, just as he must disregard everything else about Jezebel Hart that enticed him.

If he'd been in New York, he could have made her

one in a string of forgettable encounters, a simple satisfying of a body's needs in a vain attempt to soothe a restless heart that was weary and sick to death of the constant struggle.

But he wasn't in New York. Their paths would cross again and again in this tiny town.

And he'd already made a futile effort to put her out of his mind.

Their night together rushed back in, so vivid that he stumbled as he neared the tangle of vines he'd been trimming when she'd arrived. The protective barriers he'd erected crumbled, and he was suddenly right back there with her, lost in the curvaceous body, the generous heart, the teasing eyes that transformed a search for escape from relentless grief into an oasis where he found not only succor for his body but passion and…fun. He'd forgotten about fun. Couldn't recall the last time he'd laughed before a maddening, too-friendly, too-sexy siren had charged into his misery with an invitation and a dare.

Those stolen moments with her had been etched on his brain like acid, and each time he'd seen her, she'd refused to become ordinary. Invisible.

Worse even than her powerful allure was the crime he'd tried hardest to erase: she'd cradled his head to her bosom and given him ease. Shoved the endless loneliness away.

Sure, he wanted to crawl right back between her thighs and find out if he'd imagined the glory of her, but even worse, he hungered for that respite, that blessed sense of peace. Of hope that, one day, grief would let him be.

That was Jezebel's unforgivable sin, and the reason he had to get the hell out of Dodge as soon as possible. Before he could falter again.

He had to resist her. Her sin counted as nothing against his own.

Ruthlessly, he hacked at the vines he'd ripped from the tangle, discovering for himself how they were eating away at the once-white picket fence.

I always swore that one day I'd have a real house, with a white picket fence and babies and puppies and kittens.

If any utterance had the power to send him running, that one was it. What an irony that a woman who appeared more suited to a seraglio would have a craving to be June Cleaver.

He was done with that life, that dream.

In that instant, he realized that all he had to do was allow Jezebel to have the cottage, and she'd handle everything, fix it all up. He'd never have to come back to this place. Wouldn't have his heart battered by the memory of his failings.

He went stock-still and scanned his surroundings.

Sought to steel himself against what this homestead meant to him, how much of himself he'd invested in every square inch of earth.

But the roots of a dead love bound him here still, and he would have to sever them as he'd sliced at these vines. The idea nearly brought him to his knees.

Then his gaze landed on Jezebel, clasping a rose cane, her head cocked to one side and, he could swear, her mouth moving as if she were talking to the bush. With a slight gnawing of her lower lip, she made the cut and gingerly laid the cane on the ground instead of dropping it.

Again she repeated the sequence, appearing to be hurt by each cut and murmuring thanks when she finished.

The gesture should have been ludicrous, but it was oddly moving. If ever he required proof of how she would cherish this place that held pieces of his soul, he had it now.

Maybe he couldn't yet sunder his attachment to his home, but he could begin the process. He crossed halfway toward where Jezebel stood but couldn't manage the rest.

He spoke in a rush before he could change his mind.

"I'll let you have the cottage."

She froze. Slowly, she faced him, her eyes huge and equal parts fear and hope. "You'll sell it to me?"

"Rent it." He couldn't do more just now. "That's all I can promise."

Her smile was a summer's sun, every bit as blinding. "Oh, Gamble, I promise you I'll be a good steward of it. You'll never have to worry a second." She began a little jig, then faltered. "Are you sure this is okay for you? I couldn't bear it if my happiness caused you more pain."

He wasn't, but her joy made him wish to keep that smile shining. "I'm fine."

She beamed and hugged him hard, then bestowed a kiss to what should have been his cheek.

But it landed at the edge of his mouth.

Both of them jolted at the hammer blow of memory.

He stilled, and their lips were only a breath apart, her eyes wide and uncertain.

His chest was tight, everything in him suspended.

But so aware of her. Of how she lightened his heart. Her kindness, her giving.

Close, so close she was, that sense of hope, of sunshine and laughter, of strength and resilience when he was held together with the faintest of threads.

Too much in her called to him. He narrowed the gap and brushed his lips over hers, soaking up the life in her, the warmth he so sorely needed.

As their lips met in a kiss more chaste than seductive, he began to register her lush body against his, the lure of her bright spirit reaching inside him. He tightened his arms around her back, seeking. Settled her along the length of him.

Felt the urge to groan at how good she felt.

She leaned into him, gave one tiny, breathy moan—

He took her mouth then as he'd wanted to a hundred times since they'd made love, those wide, delicious lips that had the power to dissolve all rational thought. He yielded the fight to resist her, just for a minute.

Just one, then he'd—

But one became two, and her hands slipped into his hair. Against his chest, the abundant softness of her breasts. One arm encircled her waist and that hand slid down her curvaceous hips, pressing her into him.

He did groan, then, and angled his head to go deeper into the silken warmth of her mouth, while he wrapped her braid round and round his other wrist to anchor her in place.

And all the while, inside him was an ocean's roaring, waves crashing against the stones of his heart and drowning out the sounds of anything beyond the stunning demand to have this woman. He gripped her harder, and she responded with a passion that almost obscured everything else.

But in the tiny pause between one wave and the next, his conscience began to whisper.

Until finally, he heard it.

He broke away with a gasp. What was he doing, all but devouring Jezebel right here, at Charlotte's house? "No." He backed off. "I can't."

Her eyes were huge and dark with passion, and she blinked as if emerging from a spell. "Wha—"

He looked around himself for answers. "Not here. Not where—" He wheeled to escape what he'd done.

She caught his hand, and when he tried to shake her off, she only clasped tighter, pulling him to face her. "Shh, it's okay. I understand."

"Let me go," he said, as if he did not possess the greater strength by far.

"Come with me," she entreated, drawing him slowly but firmly into the shade of a stately oak, murmuring a steady stream of soothing sounds, all of them words he couldn't hear for the tumult inside his mind. "It's okay, Gamble."

"You don't get it." Misery made his voice savage. "I want you to go."

"I will, but not like this. Just sit with me a second." She tugged at him with the clear expectation that he could do nothing to refuse her.

He gathered his wits and yanked his hand from hers. "No. Get the hell away."

"Gamble." It was the voice that could quiet a rowdy bar, not loud, but calmly insistent on his attention. "I'm not going to leave you believing you've done something wrong."

He stared at her. "You don't have a clue what I'm thinking."

She went on as if he hadn't spoken. "We're attracted to each other, powerfully so. It's not criminal." She glanced up from where she sat on the grass. "And it doesn't have to be serious. You still eat, don't you?"

"What?"

"You eat food. You drink water. You even have a beer. You walk in the sunshine. Talk to other people. Charlotte can't do any of those things. Do you stop all of them?"

Fury blinded him. "Don't speak her name."

Spots of color flared in her cheeks, but she rose to stand and pressed on. "I know I'm not her, and I'm definitely no saint. Feel free to keep reminding me of that, just in case I ever manage to forget." Her voice took on a bitter cast, and he realized that he'd never heard that tone from her.

Hands on hips, she stood inches away from him. "You're a male in his prime, and your body requires more than mere food and water. You were once totally alive—" She flung out a hand. "As this place clearly demonstrates." Then she pinned him with her own anger. "The crime is to stop living, to rob the people around you of the man who could create this beauty, who could live life so richly. I don't have to know Charlotte personally to understand that she'd be the first to tell you to climb out of that grave that's not big enough for both of you."

"Don't you dare—"

But she spoke over him. "I will dare and be damned for doing so, I'm sure, but you've already tried and convicted me as the harlot who lured you away from your saintly devotion to a woman I'll never measure up to." She paused for one quick breath. "Well, screw you for making me feel worthless. I may be no Charlotte Smith, but at least I'm not a coward. Life throws crap at all of us, and you got a raw deal, but you're not the only person who ever suffered. Get over yourself."

Her eyes shone with tears she swiped at angrily. With awkward strides, she left him and began gathering her things while he watched in stunned silence.

Halfway to her car, she halted but didn't turn. "I meant to be your friend," she said stiffly, "but it's obvious that I'm the last person you'll consider worthy, so have it your way. Goodbye."

Then she left him in the echoing silence.

CHAPTER TWELVE

SKEETER HAD SENSED something was wrong, so Jezebel had to cut short her visit or risk crying again. She would shed no more tears for Gamble Smith. Hurt had pushed her to strike back at him, and she was ashamed of herself, but she hadn't said anything he didn't need to hear.

From now until he left town, she'd be courteous if she were forced to see him, but otherwise, she'd avoid him.

And do her best to forget him.

Please, she thought, but she wasn't sure what to hope for. *On fire* didn't begin to describe her body's response when he touched her. She'd never experienced anything like it.

And he had, too, blast him, even if he fought it.

All in all, she had to hope that broken condom was simply that, a torn piece of latex, and not a harbinger of sure trouble for both of them.

Even if she'd already begun to think about

learning to knit and sighed over pictures of babies in magazines.

Wrong time, wrong man, Jezebel.

Then she pondered the cottage and the lightning-fast glimpse she'd had of herself playing on the grass with a chubby-cheeked infant. He'd never rent it to her now, and that was that.

She loaded her arms with bags of groceries and went inside to pet the dog and cat who, unlike Gamble Smith, considered her pretty special.

"TAKE THE AFTERNOON OFF, Gamble. You're going to drive away customers with that frown," Lily said.

He glanced up from where he was deadheading flowers. "I was gone all morning."

She crouched beside him. "Were you at the cottage?"

He shook his head impatiently. "It doesn't matter."

She stroked his shoulder. "It does. Maybe you should let that hussy buy it."

"She's not a hussy," he snapped, only too aware of the hypocrisy of his defense.

She goggled at him. "Has she said something to you? Maybe I should pay her a visit and tell her—"

"Whoa, sis." But he smiled a little at her protective attitude, though it was more likely Jezebel who needed shielding from him.

Well, screw you, Gamble Smith, for making me feel worthless.

He snorted. Or maybe not.

You're not the only person who ever suffered.

"Lil?"

"Yes?"

"Am I—" He didn't finish; he could guess the answer. "I've been a real pain in the ass, haven't I?"

"You've been grieving over a terrible loss."

Get over yourself.

He'd been trying to do that, and in New York, he'd been making progress, but being back here...

Enough. "I have a better idea. You take the afternoon off."

Lily blinked. "Me?"

"Yeah." He tugged at a lock of her hair. "How long's it been since you ditched class?"

Her eyes twinkled. "That would be, oh, the day before graduation."

Gamble chuckled. "Why am I not surprised? Had to get in one last act of truancy, huh?"

She shrugged. "Things got too boring when all of you left home. I was trying to uphold the family rep."

"Mom catch you?"

Her smile was wide. "Nope."

"Good girl." He wrapped one arm around her

shoulders and walked her to the door of the office. "Go do something girly—a manicure or whatever."

"Gamble." She rolled her eyes and held out both hands. "A nurseryman has no nails to manicure." Hers were very short and encrusted with dirt.

"How 'bout a pedicure, *chère?* Some kinda scarlet on your toes." Cal strolled in from the nearest greenhouse. "Then me, I pick you up for dinner and you wear some of those heels that make grown men weep. Preferably with a real short skirt. After, you and I go dancin'."

"It's not appropriate for management and employees to date," Lily sniffed.

"That's okay, sugar. I wasn't askin' your mama."

She narrowed her eyes, and Gamble was torn between amusement and decking the guy for having the nerve to proposition his baby sister. The jittery pleasure in Lily's expression called for a bit of both. "I'll be spending the evening with Mom," he told her. "You go ahead. And you—" he spoke to Cal "—watch yourself."

Cal nodded to him, man to man. Then his serious expression flared into devilment again. "I'd rather watch Miss Lily here." He grinned. "'Cept she can't take her eyes off me. It gets sorta embarrassin', bein' an object of worship."

Gamble could practically see Lily's temper bashing at the inside of her skull.

"I'm outta here," she said to Gamble, then eyed Cal. "But I'll be doing something much more interesting than a pedicure."

"Be still, my heart." Cal patted his chest. "Can't wait for the results."

"You'll be waiting a long time, Calvin." She drew his name out for maximum effect, then flounced away.

His laughter followed her. "Pick you up at seven, *chère.*" He turned to Gamble. "Quite a woman, your sister. *Le bon Dieu* did a mighty fine thing the day He created the fairer sex. Nothin' like a woman in a temper to stir a man's juices." He was chuckling as he ambled off.

Gamble stared into the distance, recalling another woman departing in anger, yes, but brought on by hurt.

Stir a man's juices, indeed. She did that, far too easily; his explosive response to her unnerved him.

But she was wrong about one thing, and he wondered if he was a big enough man to tell her that she wasn't the one he'd tried and convicted as being unworthy.

That judgment he reserved for himself.

"Can you help me over here?" A customer's voice yanked him from his musings.

Gratefully, he abandoned his thoughts and went to discuss geraniums.

BUT EVEN AFTER he'd closed the nursery, showered and visited his mother, he couldn't get Jezebel off his mind. He prowled the rooms like a caged wolf. She turned him inside out, and he didn't like it one bit.

Because he liked her too much, though he suspected she'd be stunned to hear it, given his behavior.

He was only marginally cheered by the news that his mother might be allowed to go home in a week or so. He would have been more encouraged about his prospects for leaving Three Pines had not his talk with the nurse made him aware that his mom would need help at home for the next few weeks, including someone to drive her back and forth to physical therapy over in Tyler.

So he'd left a message for Kat that no new work would be forthcoming for a while, but even as he said the words, his fingers began to itch to pick up a brush again. He still had supplies in his studio, but he wasn't eager to return to the cottage.

There was no cure for his restlessness until he squared things with Jezebel.

Thus it was that he found himself parked behind the bar, deep in the shadows beneath the branches of an ancient oak, waiting for the last of the customers to leave, so he could talk to her without a crowd.

His day had been long, and he nearly nodded off before she appeared. When she did, he could tell she

didn't realize she wasn't alone; she made no effort
to hide her weariness. He'd witnessed her spreading
cheer and spitting mad, but this dispirited woman
was new…and disturbing. She worked hard, but he
might have played a part in the slump of her shoulders.

He emerged from the truck, and the sound of his
footsteps on gravel had her whirling, alarm on her face.

"It's only me, Jezebel." He moved into the moonlight.

Exhaustion became wariness. "Why are you here?"

He expelled a breath. "Good question." He took a
step toward her. "I owe you an apology, but you seem
tired. It can wait."

She frowned. "An apology for what?"

"How about being a bastard to you, for starters?
For making you cry?"

She shrugged off his claim. "I said some things I
shouldn't have."

He neared and was disquieted to see her retreat,
one hand on the screen door. "I suspect you only
voiced what a lot of other people would like to." He
glanced away and shook his head, weary himself.
"There are things I've never told anyone about Charlotte and me, the day she—" His throat tightened.

She placed a hand on his arm. "You don't owe me
that, Gamble. I'm sorry I was so insensitive. It's

obvious you loved her deeply, and I have no right to presume what you should be doing now."

There it was again, the kind heart inside a bombshell's body. The sex goddess was tough to resist, but this woman was lethal.

And he was so damn lonely.

"I was furious with her for getting pregnant. She understood it was too risky." Ire rose in him again. "I should never have left birth control up to her, but she was determined that I not get a vasectomy, so that I could have children if anything—" He had to stop and swallow. "There was too much about her health that she couldn't control, and she promised—" He struggled to keep the bitterness out of his voice. "She thanked me…and then played me for a fool. Once it was too late, she was ecstatic. She believed we would be even happier if our family was complete, regardless that I'd told her a thousand times or more that she was all I ever wanted."

Jezebel's expression was mingled sympathy and misery.

"Don't feel sorry for me, damn it. I couldn't forgive her, couldn't be happy about it. I made an effort, but I was scared to death of losing her. That last day I went to pick up the crib I'd built her as a surprise, but I never told her—" He realized his hands were clenched. "She died believing I was angry and, goddammit, I still am. She had no right—"

But even as he said the words he'd contemplated over and over again, he realized that the usual rage in them was missing. Instead, he felt only…empty. Lost.

For so long, grief and anger had been his closest companions.

Now he was just…tired.

"Come inside, Gamble." She slid her hand down and clasped his. "Let me make you some tea."

He laughed, but there was no humor in it. "You are really a sucker for a lost cause, aren't you?" And he realized that he didn't even care that he was just one more of her charity cases. She was a burning torch in a dark world, and he didn't want to be left with his thoughts anymore.

Then he remembered the papers in his pocket. "Here."

"What is this?"

"A lease agreement."

"Oh, Gamble…I don't think this is a good idea."

"Why not? Changed your mind because I ruined it for you?"

"No, it's only—" She peered up at him. "I'm not willing to cause you hurt. I'll manage something." She handed them back. "I don't belong there."

"You're wrong." He tilted her chin. "Once that

JEAN BRASHEAR 203

place was a little bit of heaven, and the only part that's changed is me. You nailed it when you said that it was meant to be lived in and loved. I just can't be the one to do it anymore, but you can. You and that big, crazy heart of yours." He shoved the papers back at her.

But turmoil crowded her gaze.

"What? You really don't want it?"

She shook her head. "That's not it."

"Tell me."

But she turned away, her shoulders slumped in defeat, though he couldn't imagine why. He yielded to impulse and drew her into his arms. She was stiff at first, but then she clung to him.

"What's wrong, Jezebel?"

She still didn't speak. He tilted her face to his and saw two fat tears roll down her cheeks.

"It seems I am forever making you cry." He pressed his lips to first one eyelid, then the other, moved by her sorrow.

He trailed kisses down to her mouth, but this time, instead of devouring, he only rubbed his lips softly against hers. A small sob ended in a sigh of pleasure, and he sought to soothe her even as he ached to feast.

"Would you like to come inside?" she whispered. "No strings, I promise."

She was so clearly a woman for attachment and

commitment. It wasn't right or fair to take her up on her promise—

But he wanted her so badly—her body, yes, but even more…her sweetness.

He vowed to make it good for her, even as he knew himself for a man who didn't deserve her.

He lifted her into his arms.

Jezebel sighed once more. "I always dreamed of someone doing that, but I'm too big." She tensed. "You should put me down. Don't hurt your back."

"My back isn't what's aching." He quieted her with another kiss as he strode through the door and kicked it closed with his foot.

And nearly fell over the dog dancing beneath them.

"Oh—I'm sorry. Rufus needs to go out." She scrambled down, her face fiery red. "Oh, man. Are you okay?"

He realized he could still laugh. "I'm fine. I'll take him. Will he run away?"

"You don't have to do that."

He cupped her cheek and stole a taste of her. "Then we'll go together."

And they did.

"A highly recommended way to seduce a man," she said, as they watched Rufus nose his way from tree to tree. "Break his back, then his leg, then set him to watching your dog pee."

His mouth twitched. "I have to admit that it's original. Not one woman I met in Manhattan ever thought of this method." He bent to her. "You might have to get on top, seeing as how I've lost the use of my back and legs."

"Oh, jeez." She covered her face.

Gamble laughed and the sound of it startled him. "You are a fraud," he said.

"What?"

"You're a Victorian maiden inside the body of a vixen. How on earth do you survive running a bar?"

She shrank visibly. "I've done worse." She pivoted as if ready to run. "I think we'd better say goodnight now. Rufus, come here."

"Wait—" He grabbed her arm. "What just happened?"

"Nothing. Go home."

"Not until you explain."

"It isn't you." At last, she faced him. "I'm no maiden, Gamble. I used to be a stripper. My body has been all that stood between me and starvation sometimes, so I used it." Her stance dared him to sneer. "I was orphaned at five, on the street at thirteen. I never finished school. Light-years from someone like Charlotte." She yanked her arm from his grasp. "I'd like you to leave now, please."

Such exquisite politeness.

"No."

Her head jerked up. "You assume the fact that I've used my body before entitles you to it? Well, you're wrong. I fought my way out of the gutter, and I'm not going back. I'm never letting any man touch me again just to get his rocks off. Not unless it's my idea."

She was magnificent in her furious vulnerability. "How about to express admiration?"

Her eyes went to slits. "Men have ogled my figure forever."

"I'm not talking about your figure, though I won't deny it can make a guy break into a cold sweat." He captured her hand. She hissed, but he refused to release her.

Instead, he raised it to his lips, keeping his eyes locked on hers. "Your experiences could have made you hard, but they haven't. You did what was required for you to survive, but it hasn't tarnished that big heart of yours. You shame me, Jezebel. I've never lacked for love, while you had no one, yet you spread affection as if it were water, freely available and endless in supply." He pressed his mouth to her skin, then let go and stepped away. "I'll say good night, but I won't have you believing it's because you're the one who comes up short." He bent to kiss her cheek. "Sweet dreams." He turned to leave, though everything in him yearned to stay.

JEZEBEL STOOD FROZEN, her mind a dizzying whirl of emotions. He was a troubled man, and her life was complicated enough.

But something in him called to her. Lured her.

And thoroughly confused her.

He said he admired her in spite of hearing about her past. Few details, of course, but she hadn't spared the worst of it. He knew her body had been displayed for grasping men in seedy bars. That she had no education, that no one wanted her—

He believed he was the unworthy one. Was concerned enough for her to walk away.

"Wait."

He halted but didn't turn.

She gnawed at her lip.

Took the first step. "Don't leave, Gamble."

He glanced back at her. "Don't feel sorry for me, Jezebel."

"I don't."

"Then why?"

"Maybe I'm lonely, too."

He tensed. "I never said I was."

"You didn't have to." They regarded each other in silence. She frowned. "I don't understand what this is between us."

A rueful smile. "Some of it's pretty clear." His gaze held her in place. He shook his head. "But heat isn't enough for you. You're not meant for careless nights of sweaty sex."

"I told you no strings."

"You're a strings kind of girl, honey."

"Then show me tenderness, Gamble. Forget tomorrow. Don't imagine I'm expecting a lifetime. I'm not. We're both adults, and we know you're leaving. You've got bigger things in store."

The silence thrummed with the seductive bass notes of promise.

"One night, not as strangers this time but as friends. Two people who have no future as anything else."

He stared at her, clearly torn.

"Let's shove away the darkness together. I won't ask for more, I swear it." She was tired of caution and planning and being strong and responsible. Even if she was pregnant, she expected nothing from him. She spread her arms. "Make me hot, Gamble. Burn with me. Let's both go a little haywire tonight. Tomorrow we'll be sensible again." And she discovered a smile that was genuine. "Let's play. When's the last time you just fooled around?"

She could see the temptation in him and found her way to more certain footing. He'd been responsible for an invalid since he was little more than a child himself, then he'd suffered a terrible loss and had been grieving ever since. She could give him this, and grant herself the boon, as well.

She could do so because she was strong enough to deal with the fallout all on her own. It sure wouldn't be the first time.

And she had come to care about this man. She wouldn't walk away unscathed when it was time for him to go, no, but life, she'd discovered long ago, was as much about scars as pretty sunsets and flowers. The trick was in honoring both.

He still didn't move.

The balloon of her daring deflated. "You're not interested." Humiliation crawled up her throat. "No problem. I'll just—" She let her arms drop. "I'm going inside. Drive safely." She made her way toward the door.

Two steps later, he captured her. Swung her around, pupils so dark they swallowed the blue. Suppressed hunger vibrated in his frame, and her own body flared to answering heat.

"I want you, but—" His jaw snapped shut. He began again. "I'm not sure if I can be tender. Not at first. You make me crazy, Jezebel."

Her eyes closed in mingled thanksgiving and nerves. Then she opened them. "Who says I'll be gentle with you?"

Blue flame leaped. Suddenly, she was in his arms,

and his fingers tangled in her hair. His mouth raced over her throat, while his free hand caressed one breast with touches so feather-light that she had the urge to clamp her own over his and beg. She wrapped one leg around his thighs and undulated against him.

He groaned and nipped at her collarbone. She swallowed a moan. She craved to crawl up his body, to shred the control he was struggling to maintain. To drive him out of his mind and lose her own with him.

He beat her to it. Gripped her hips in his hands and lifted her to the truck's hood. Clasped her thighs and parted them. Moved inside.

Jezebel reclined on her elbows, her limbs loose and languid. Gamble's fingers grazed under her gauzy blouse and bared skin as he traveled. His tongue swirled around her navel, and her body arched on a gasp.

He chuckled and skimmed a damp trail beneath her waistband even as his fingers busied themselves with her zipper, a slow, torturous slide made agonizing as he blew tendrils of breath over damp skin. She shivered.

Then he stopped. "Your hair," he said hoarsely. "I want it loose." He worked at her braid, swiftly untangling it, then unbuttoned her blouse and popped the front catch of her bra. He draped her hair over her shoulders until it covered her breasts, leaving her disheveled and half-naked in the spill of moonlight.

His gaze painted over her, as physical as a caress.

"You are the most stunning creature I have ever laid my eyes on." His grin was quick and lethal. "I can't figure out where to taste first."

"Then it's my turn." She levered herself to sitting, grasped the hem of his T-shirt and raked her hands up his chest, carrying the fabric with her. She bent to nip at his abs, swirl her own tongue around the length of one rib.

He jumped and...*giggled*. That was the only word for it.

Jezebel smiled. "Ticklish." She slicked up his side, and he jerked away so fast she nearly fell.

"Stop that."

She had his shirt in her hand and paused to relish at the picture he made, a barbarian cast in shadows and starlight. "Make me."

That set the tone.

They would play. Have fun.

His eyes narrowed. He scooped her up and threw her over his shoulder. Her hair swept the ground. He twirled them both until she was dizzy. Paused, and the ground spun.

Before she could unscramble her brain, she felt

her jeans slip down her legs and drop into the dust with a soft plop. "Gamble—"

His hands caressed her bottom, and skillful fingers slipped beneath her panties—

Jezebel lost whatever she'd been about to say. Need roared over her, an insane tangle of urges she couldn't sort out. "Gamble, let me—"

His tongue trailing the line of muscle in her thigh silenced her again. "Oh."

Next thing she knew, she was sliding down the front of him, her legs parting around his waist. "You're strong," she marveled. "That makes me unbelievably hot. Now, put me down."

A slash of white teeth. "Uh-uh. Hold on."

She scarcely managed to grasp his shoulders in time, as his arms descended to her hips, and her upper body fell backward.

In the gap he'd created between them, he swooped in and clamped his mouth on one breast.

"Dear, sweet—" Jezebel's mouth dried up. All she could do was hang on for the ride.

And a ride it was. Gamble walked them back to the truck hood and laid her out like a banquet. He began to ease away, but her legs tightened around his hips. He hooked a finger in her bikini panties. One eyebrow arched.

"Oh, yeah. I always wished someone would do that, too."

He ripped her panties from her with a smile that would light up the sky.

Then he dove between her legs, and Jezebel saw stars.

Gamble lost himself in pleasuring her, finding a patience he hadn't expected, even as his body twanged like a too-taut bowstring about to snap. Her skin was a feast, her curves a banquet, her hair a glory. Draped in abandon over the hood of a pickup, she was a Gypsy queen with raven tresses, a siren calling men to dash themselves on rocks.

Dear heaven, what a subject for a painting she would be.

He couldn't get enough of her.

When her scream died off to a long, low moan and her arms flung outward in surrender, he pressed one more slow, wet kiss to the crease of her leg and rose.

"I can't move." Her nipples were hard, her flesh was covered in goose pimples, and she was smiling.

"Don't try." He could almost forget, in the magnificence of her, that his own body was aching.

Then she pounced. In a blur, she was on him, dragging him close and tearing at his jeans. "Gotcha," she crowed. "Your turn." She dropped to her knees and put her mouth on him.

His eyes rolled back in his head. He lingered in the stun-force spell until his body overheated into the red zone.

Then he yanked her up. "Uh-uh." As swiftly as he could manage with a brain fogged by lust, he hitched her back to the truck, covered himself and drove into her.

She yelped, and he halted in alarm, hardly breathing.

Then her head lolled back, and she made a guttural sound that was unmistakably pleasure.

He fastened his teeth on her throat and thrust again. "Yes-s-s-s."

He began to chuckle, but her inner muscles tightened, and his laughter became a groan.

She rose, clenched his hair and slanted her mouth on his.

And everything went a little crazy just about then.

Jezebel felt it when Gamble let his guard fall. A glimpse of his face in the dappled moonlight opened up a place inside her that she knew would forever be unavailable to anyone else. The lines of pain dissolved, and the haunted hollows ebbed, however temporarily. He was all about hunger, but even so, tenderness coated each gesture, melting her insides like hot, sweet wax.

He was a far better man than he allowed himself to believe.

Heartache would come for her somewhere not far down the road. He wouldn't want her to care so much, she was certain.

She couldn't help it. Wouldn't, if she could. She'd been kidding herself, of course, that tonight was only about fun. Some moments were too precious to be casual.

Even if some hearts had no future together.

Tonight he was here, and tomorrow would have to take care of tomorrow.

For now…she would revel.

CHAPTER THIRTEEN

I WAS HOPING I'd imagined how good it was before.

And this time was even better.

Gamble waited for the inevitable guilt to creep over him, for so long now his most constant companion.

But Jezebel tossed her arms wide. "Wow."

And she began to laugh like a loon.

For a split second, he felt grief beckon him, demanding his attention, scraping over his nerves like nettles—

But Jezebel lifted her head just then, eyes sparkling in the moonlight, her face wreathed in smiles and fun and—

She's so sturdy, he marveled. He'd practically ravished her like some pirate, and she'd taken everything he could dish out—

And done some dishing of her own.

Her enthusiasm, her sheer joy in living, was a lifeboat to a drowning man, a shimmering pool of water amid barren sands.

Just as her grin began to slip, he met it with one of his own, surprised that his was genuine.

"Yeah. Double wow."

Hers flared once more, and he was caught yet again by her innate sweetness. Life had done a number on her every bit as much as it had on him, yet she'd chosen to meet it head-on, to scrap her way toward a better future without losing her cheer in the process.

"I can't believe you giggled when I tickled you."

"Guys don't giggle."

She rose, one eyebrow arched, fingers flexing in implied threat. "Oh, yes, indeed. Like a little, bitty girl." One hand darted toward his side, and Gamble leaped backward so fast he stumbled.

Jezebel threw back her head and laughed, belly-deep.

And Gamble could only stop and stare. She was magnificent. An Amazon queen, naked and glistening, strong and indomitable and so damn beautiful she could halt the breath in your chest.

A fleeting wisp of thought, comparing her with his gentle, timid Charlotte, he ruthlessly rejected.

"Keep your distance," he commanded.

"What? You're scared of me now?" She descended from the hood and advanced on him with long, confident strides. "That's probably healthy. You do seem to have an impressive number of sensitive spots on you." Her expression was pure mischief.

"I'll show you sensitive," he growled. He scooped her up and fastened his teeth to her throat.

A swift gasp was his reward as he strode to her front door and quickly crossed to her bedroom, abandoning their clothes all over the ground outside.

The idea made him smile.

And then there were no more thoughts. Only sighs and murmurs, moans and whispers as body brushed body, heat melded to heat and Gamble lost himself in Jezebel's sweetness.

THE FOLLOWING HOURS were the most carefree he could remember in years.

He left Jezebel's bed reluctantly in the morning, aware that others were still pulling too much of his load. He gathered their clothes from outside, shook out as much dirt as he could and donned his own. Set hers inside and yielded to temptation long enough to nuzzle her half-awake.

She rolled from where she'd sprawled on her stomach next to him and blinked a drowsy smile. Her eyes lighting at the sight of him was a gift he would take with him. "Hi."

"Hi, yourself."

"What time is it?"

"Early. Go on back to sleep. You didn't get much."

"Yeah." The smile slipped into smugness. Then her gaze cleared a little. "You didn't, either."

"Yeah." As much a sigh as a statement. He shook his head. "But the nursery beckons." He hesitated, uncertain about what happened next.

"I might need to buy some flowers later," she said.

Gratitude that she would make it easy raced over him. "I have an idea where you could get some." He traced one of the wild tresses spread over her shoulder and barely resisted the urge to continue the path over her skin.

Her breath hitched, and her eyes were an answering gratitude.

But neither of them seemed to know what to say, the joy of the last several hours caught in a nexus of uncertain future and uneasy past.

He cleared his throat. "I was thinking that I could help you some with the—" He shrugged. "The cleanup at the—" He didn't want to bring the cottage and its attendant memories front and center just yet, but he was aware of a drive to spend time with her out of bed.

Her gaze sparked. "So you'll still—" She pressed her lips together. The same reluctance appeared to exist within her.

He swallowed hard. The path out of his dark place

was enveloped in brambles. He wasn't sure he had what it would take to emerge.

But he had to start somewhere.

"Yes." He focused on her like a lodestar.

Her expression relaxed some. "I'll be there all afternoon, then." She rose to sitting and grasped the covers. "I'll walk you out."

"No." He pushed gently on her shoulder until she lay back again. He heard the huskiness in his voice. "Let me remember you like this." He dropped a light kiss on her lips, and tore himself away before he wound up right back in there with her.

He was nearly to the bedroom door when he paused. Gripped the jamb. "Thank you," he said.

And didn't look back as he left.

THANK YOU. The words echoed long after as Jezebel found herself unable to sleep, energized by the night. She leaped from the bed, noted the bright sunlight pouring through the two small front windows and absorbed the sight of her folded clothes from last night on a table by the door.

And couldn't resist a little happy-dance that had Rufus barking and Oscar hissing in annoyance.

To feel this much joy over one simple night was absurd.

Except it hadn't been simple. It had been… amazing. Stunning. Rock-my-world hot.

Ooh, how every last inch of her was replete with a staggering satiation, sinfully rich, gloriously…juicy. She was almost ready to come out of her skin at the mere notion of all they'd done together in the dark.

Or the moonlight. She hugged herself and grinned.

The hood of a pickup. That only happened in steamy novels.

"Nope," she told Rufus, holding his front paws as he stood and tried to dance with her, slobbering his adoration. "It happened right here in Three Pines, boy. To me—" She released his paws and jabbed a thumb toward her chest.

And laughed deliriously while Rufus barked.

She put water on to boil and headed for the bathroom, detouring long enough to soothe Oscar's pout. She began the shower, then opened the medicine cabinet to grab toothpaste—

And spotted the pregnancy test kit.

Her spirits plummeted.

She dropped her toothbrush in the sink and folded to the floor opposite.

Today was the day, the first one she could expect an answer. She buried her head in her arms.

She didn't have to take the test; she could simply wait and see if her period started. She was fairly regular; it would only be two or three days before she'd have an inkling.

The appeal of the reprieve was altogether too inviting. She would have more time to find out what might develop between her and Gamble without the burden of such an immense—and emotional—complication.

Coward.

Her mouth quirked. She was every bit that, she admitted.

But she was also worried about Gamble. He had hazarded a crucial step across a very fragile bridge this morning. She'd felt the tension of grief pulling at him even as he dared to venture into a new future.

If she was pregnant, that news would send him tumbling into the treacherous ravine of his past.

But she might not be, and then the way would be clear—

For what? He's leaving. And you told him you understood that. There's no place in that life for you.

She did understand. And she was fully prepared to cope with both his leaving and any legacy of that first night. She would even tell him about the baby—

When he was ready.

Right now, he was not. He'd laughed. Giggled, for Pete's sake. How could she rob him of the chance to extend his venture into the light? That flame would be extinguished, maybe forever, if she even hinted at a suspicion of a pregnancy, and she understood herself well enough to be certain that she could never keep a secret of such magnitude for long.

A few days wouldn't hurt anyone, and she was too scared of forcing him back into that dark place if what she suspected was true.

The best way to shield him was not to know herself.

So Jezebel rose, grabbed the test kit and stashed it in the under-sink cabinet, and attempted to do the same with the seed in her mind.

Gamble Smith needed laughter and fun worse than anyone she'd ever met. She couldn't have his love, and she might not have his presence long.

But they could enjoy stolen days together, as many as fate allowed them.

She pulled aside the shower curtain and made ready to grab whatever hours she could wrest from fate's greedy fingers.

GAMBLE APPROACHED the cottage and his palms were slick with sweat, yes, but his chest didn't feel quite so tight as before. He'd made a decision, and he would stick by it, even if there was still a ball of ice in his stomach.

His rational mind told him it was time to move on. A part of him even yearned to be freed from the quicksand of remorse, but he'd lost faith that he deserved any joy.

He still had no idea how to put behind him the way he and Charlotte had parted, but Jezebel had been right when she'd accused him of dishonoring what he and Charlotte had created by letting it slide into ruin.

You may not be able to see the end of the road, but you can see the next step. When it's all you've got, that's what you do—take that next step, then another. How often had his mother said that?

His mother had more courage in her little finger than he possessed in his whole body, based on how he'd conducted himself thus far.

His road ahead was murky, but he could manage this one try. He drove through the gate and looked around for Jezebel. Noted that she had the flowerbeds in front of the porch already cleared of weeds previously choking the azaleas, loaded with buds ready to burst into bloom. She'd obviously been hard at work, all the more impressive for how little sleep he'd allowed her last night.

Suddenly, he heard the sound of a dog's furious barking—

And a woman's scream.

He shut off the engine and charged to the rear of the cottage like a madman.

Skidded to a halt at the sight before him.

And couldn't help but chuckle.

Jezebel was shrieking—but her shouts were of laughter, belly-deep. She'd managed to acquire streaks of dirt over most of her clothing and nearly every patch of skin, and she was attempting to wash them off with water from the hose.

But her dog, huge and golden, was bounding toward the stream of water and snapping at it as if it posed a serious danger to his mistress, getting himself drenched in the process…and shaking off all the excess on her.

Once again she'd surprised him. Most women would have been upset and scolding the dog while doing whatever was necessary to dodge getting themselves dirty.

But not Jezebel. Her hair was dripping wet and her hat had been flung to the ground nearby, its brim crumpled by both her feet and the dog's as she danced around him, squirting the water as he barked and frolicked with her.

She glanced up and spotted Gamble. The stream from the hose followed the path of her gaze.

Soaking his shirt in the process.

"Oops." Her eyes widened. "Sorry. Rufus and I were just—"

Spurred by an extraordinary impulse he couldn't explain, Gamble leaped toward her and wrested the hose from her grip. "Sorry, huh? I just changed my shirt."

He aimed the spray right at her.

Jezebel shrieked again as he hit her smack in the chest.

Rufus barked and raced to tackle the liquid monster. Gamble pointed the hose over his head in a teasing arc, and while he was distracted, Jezebel charged—

Slipped on the soaking-wet grass—

And took Gamble down with her.

He lost control of the hose, left whipping around like a demented snake. As soon as it settled, Rufus charged it.

Jezebel lay in the mud beneath Gamble, giggling hysterically. She was filthy, but her eyes sparkled with merriment.

And some of the ice inside his chest melted. Reflected joy flooded him.

Yes, she was a stunner, built for long nights and wet dreams, too gorgeous to be true. But what he felt most strongly at that moment was not the luscious body under his or the beautiful face beneath the grime.

It was hope, even more seductive. Light and cheer and promise that day might dawn for him again.

Jezebel fell silent, and the sound of the water and the dog faded. For a second, Gamble remembered what it was like to live in sunshine and faith. The sheer and immense pleasure of that moment had him leaning to kiss her in gratitude for the bounty of it.

He reveled in the little hum of delight that issued from her throat as she returned a curiously innocent kiss, more friendship than desire, optimism rather than a search for succor and respite.

Very soon, though, hunger surfaced. Before it could take over, Gamble ended the kiss, for once unwilling to settle for the purely physical.

Her eyes opened slowly, and he tensed, unable to explain himself or his reaction.

She rubbed one hand over his back in a comforting gesture, as though she understood. Then her gaze dropped to his chest, and her smile spread.

He glanced down and saw telltale brown streaks on his clean white T-shirt.

"Oops," she said again, with no remorse evident.

Before he could summon a response, Rufus slurped at his cheek.

"Rufus!" she warned.

Gamble rolled off her, relieved by the interruption. "Not through playing, boy?"

The dog's eyes cut to the hose, still pouring water on the ground, then back to Gamble. His tail wagged.

Memories of childhood fun had Gamble lunging for the dog, play-growling and roughhousing with him. Rufus barked with joy and tumbled into Gamble's chest.

The game was on.

Finally, he and Rufus gave out at about the same time, and Gamble flopped to his back in the light shade of a dogwood, the dog panting heavily at his side.

Gamble looked up through the spring-green leaves into the blue sky above and welcomed the pleasant feeling of exhaustion. The day was warm, his skin was cool from water and breeze and his mind was, for once, easy.

Soon he would speak to Jezebel, offer to help her clean up. Figure out how to feel about that kiss.

But right now, just for a second, he would close his eyes, content to simply…be.

JEZEBEL HAD STUDIED them while sitting in a puddle, water soaking into her jeans. All too aware of just what a wreck she was and what would be required before she could get ready to go to work tonight. She had no spare clothes with her, no towel to place on the seat of her car.

But the sound of Gamble's laughter, as free as a boy's, rendered her unable to do anything but remain where she was, for fear of interrupting him.

So this was what the old Gamble Smith had been like before tragedy had cast a shadow over him. With a wry smile, she settled back to watch a man who desperately needed to laugh wrestling with a slobbering, happy dog.

And at that moment, Jezebel Hart, for the first time in her life, fell in love.

It didn't seem to matter just now that they had no future, that he would leave and she would stay. That she might be hiding a secret.

That her heart would break, and he would never have a clue.

One kiss that could have been exchanged by young teens had managed to penetrate where the most expert lovemaking had not. One instant in which a laughing man and a barking dog and a puddle of mud had conspired to open up a wary heart that for many years had protected itself mightily.

So what was she supposed to do with all the feelings rocketing around inside her now?

She was venturing so far outside herself it was terrifying. Heartache waited, she knew, the pound of flesh demanded in exchange for an outrageous joy.

Screw it. She mentally donated a dollar to her jar as she accepted that she would hurt and hurt badly in the not-too-distant future. Gamble Smith wasn't remotely ready to return the ridiculous amount of emotion she was experiencing. To even flirt with the notion was insane.

She'd walked into this, fooling herself that she wouldn't get attached. She'd been proven wrong, but that was her problem, not his. As both Gamble and Rufus slid into slumber beneath the shade of a tree, Jezebel reminded herself that she was a big girl, and she'd survived everything else life had thrown at her.

She would manage this, too. Somehow.

She remained still until she was certain both of them were deeply asleep. Then she rose slowly and tiptoed to the faucet, turned off the water and carefully picked her way to the rear of the house. She would dearly love to take a shower, but she felt the need to proceed with caution about making herself at home in the house that was still more Charlotte's than hers. For the time being, she would do what she could with the hose in the front yard.

The disarray inside her, however, would require more than a simple application of water.

GAMBLE STARTLED AWAKE when the big head landed on his chest.

Adoring brown doggy eyes stared into his. A long tail slapped against his leg. Gamble stretched, and the dog bolted to instant attention, ready to play again.

Gamble sat up slowly, unable to recall the last time he'd slept so deeply. He noted the sun slipping near the treetops to the west and stood. "Jezebel?"

Beside him, Rufus perked his ears. Whined softly.

"Where is she, boy?" He scratched the dog's head, his own mind muzzy. Surely she wouldn't have left Rufus with him. "Let's find her." Wet cloth clung to him in the lengthening shadows, and he shivered. He started for the back door, then glanced at the mud caking his boots. He'd check the front yard for her car first.

As they rounded the side of the house, he rolled his neck and shook his head in an attempt to fully awaken, but his limbs seemed to be moving through molasses. He yawned until his jaw cracked.

He could sleep for a week.

Then he smiled, oddly refreshed, nonetheless. When he arrived, her car was still there, the front doors both open. Gamble frowned and made his way over.

Rufus charged past him with an excited yelp, and Gamble barely managed to grab his collar in time. "No!" he ordered, as quietly as he could. "Get back."

Jezebel reposed on an old scratchy blanket tossed over the seat. She was apparently asleep, but still Gamble's heart beat a little fast until he could ascertain a regular rise and fall in her chest.

Once he was sure, he gave himself a minute to simply observe. She must have washed herself off, along with her clothes, but not in the shower, he could tell. He spotted another hose lying in the grass. Her socks and outer shirt drying on a bush.

He had a perfectly good shower, washer and dryer inside; why hadn't she used them?

Even he could figure that out, when his first reaction was to flinch at the notion.

Because, you jerk, you've made it quite obvious that this house is a shrine to Charlotte.

Jezebel was far too sensitive to the moods of others and respectful of their privacy to encroach.

Gamble leaned one hand against the car's roof while petting Rufus to keep him at bay. Studied the woman before him, her frame loose in slumber, black ringlets as shiny as a crow's wing spread over the ancient blanket in disarray.

Heaven help me, you're beautiful. Bountiful in more than her figure. Kind and caring and generous.

And playful. A free spirit, as a sudden memory of her dancing through watery arcs, rainbows in the air and a gamboling dog at her feet, could attest.

Something about her lightened his heart in a way that was difficult for him to accept as his due, precisely because he wanted to so much.

"Hi." Her voice was thick and gut-tighteningly sexy.

He jerked his gaze to hers, her smile instant and genuine.

"Hi. You can't be comfortable there."

She stretched that voluptuous body, and Gamble's eyes nearly popped out of his head. She smothered a yawn as she answered, "I doubt the ground was all that soft, either."

He skimmed his glance over her clothes. "You could have showered inside."

She ducked her chin. "It was okay."

"Would you like to come in? The plumbing works, I swear, and I could loan you a T-shirt or something."

"I should head back. I have to open the bar soon, anyway."

He surprised himself by asking, "Could Darrell do it?" Her expression was equally startled. "So you could have a night off?"

"A night off?" she repeated as if he'd spoken a foreign language.

He hesitated. *Take that next step.* "Yeah. You know, like…a social life."

"What—" She cleared her throat. "What would I do?"

The words wouldn't come. He and Jezebel stared at each other.

Then he saw her begin to close in. Her gaze dropped. *Try again,* he told himself. "You could…" He swallowed hard, then rushed ahead. "Have dinner with me."

Her head jerked upward. "With…you?"

He might as well be thirteen, so awkward he felt. But at thirteen, he'd already given his heart to—
No. Not now.

Oh, God, he thought. *This is too hard.*

"Just as friends, you mean."

She'd handed him the perfect opening. *Yeah,* he started to say—

"No." He'd startled her again. "Or maybe so. Hell, I don't—"

She placed one hand on his arm. "It doesn't matter." She smiled, though it was a little uncertain. "I'd like to have dinner with you. Wednesday is a slow night, usually. I'll call Darrell and ask."

"If you tell him why, he'll say no."

She winked. "Then I guess I'd better not explain."

And there she was again, that woman who understood fun.

"If you don't want to shower here, then I'll pick you up at seven."

She flicked a glance past him to the cottage, and something skimmed over her features too quickly to catch. "I'll take Rufus home and clean up." She cast him a saucy grin. "I imagine that even though Three Pines is a little short on fine dining, I'd do well to show up in more than a clean T-shirt."

He chuckled. "The town's also a little short on good gossip right now."

"The two of us showing up together will fix that."

"I planned to go somewhere else."

"Oh." Her grin faded. "Of course."

He stepped closer. "That's not why. I just assumed you'd enjoy something besides Lorena's or the Dairy Queen."

"Sure." A new smile, somewhat forced. "That's nice of you."

He'd hurt her. Was that his fate from now on? To hurt women who deserved better? "I'm not nice, Jezebel. But I don't set out to be a bastard, either. There's a place in Tyler that might not be Manhattan but is much more interesting than anything here." He clenched his jaw. "But if you'd rather hit Lorena's so that I can prove I'm not ashamed to be seen with you, then Lorena's it is."

She tossed that godforsaken mane, and her hands fisted at her waist. "I've never been to Manhattan, but I'm also no fool, except perhaps for taking you up on this invitation. But I can't recall the last time I enjoyed a meal out, so you're on, buster." Before he could find a response, she'd snapped her fingers imperiously. "Let's go, Rufus."

The Amazon queen had chosen to reappear.

All Gamble could do was watch as she punched the accelerator and zipped off.

But at the gate, her brake lights flared. Jezebel threw open the door and seemed embarrassed. "Some exit. I forgot to put up the hoses and tools."

Gamble waved her off. "I've got it. See you in a couple of hours."

She said something he couldn't quite make out as she left.

Then it hit him. *You are too a nice person.*

Gamble shook his head and found a laugh.

And went to clean up Jezebel's mess.

CHAPTER FOURTEEN

INSANE.

She was completely, irretrievably bonkers for ever agreeing to this, Jezebel realized as she stood in front of her closet with twenty minutes left, attempting to figure out what on earth to wear for this…not-date. Why hadn't she asked for details, even the most basic clues?

Because he'd been a breath away from changing his mind. Honesty demanded that she admit that.

Why hadn't she let him? What kind of masochist was she?

Six-forty-two.

She chewed at her lip, trying to recall when she'd last been this nervous.

Someone banged on her door.

She shrieked and grabbed the nearest hanger. Yanked off the red slip dress and slicked it over her head. "Just a minute," she called out. She fumbled for shoes, then dropped the first ones. Green heels, uh, no. It wasn't Christmas.

Another knock. "I said—Oh, never mind," she muttered. "He'll just have to wait while I come back in and search some more." She nearly tripped over Rufus and paused to soothe him. "I'm fine," she told herself. "Calm, I swear it."

Even the dog knew she was lying. She yanked open the door. "You're early—"

It wasn't Gamble.

"I thought you were resting." Darrell's expression was thunderous. He held out a plate. "I made you supper."

"Oh. I, uh—"

"She's going out with me." Gamble appeared behind Darrell.

If Darrell's eyebrows drew any closer together, they'd link. "You're not sick."

"I didn't exactly say…"

"You told me you needed the night off. You never take time for yourself."

"She's doing it now," Gamble said. "You got a problem with it?"

Darrell's glare grew to encompass the other man. "Yeah. Jezebel don't date, and she shouldn't begin with you."

She waited for Gamble to protest that it wasn't a date.

He didn't. "I believe that's between Jezebel and me. Could have sworn you're married."

With a rumble, Darrell moved to close the distance between them.

Gamble didn't back down.

She darted between them. "Guys. Chill." She turned to Darrell. "I didn't lie to you. I do need a night off. You're always telling me I work too hard."

"Yeah, but—"

She cut him off. "So are you withdrawing your offer?"

"Wouldn't have made it if I'd had a clue you were going out with him."

"We're not going out. We're just—"

Gamble slipped an arm around her waist. "What we are is none of his business."

Darrell's nostrils flared, but she was too shaken by Gamble's gesture to gather her wits and clarify.

Even if she'd been sure what, exactly, she and Gamble were.

"Told you before, you hurt her, and you answer to me," Darrell said. "I understand a man grieving. I'd be lost without my Shirley. But Jezebel deserves better than a rebound."

Gamble's grip tightened. His face was frozen in

lines of strain. He didn't answer, which was telling. He was, of course, on the rebound.

But there was much more to him that Darrell didn't see.

"Darrell, I'm lucky to count you as my friend. I mean that." And she did. "But you have to trust that I know what I'm doing."

His piercing gaze finally switched from Gamble to her. "Do you?" he challenged.

No. I'm completely insane. He is *going to hurt me.*

"Yes," she answered. She mustered every ounce of conviction she could summon.

Darrell shook his head sadly. "I disagree, but you ain't listening." His shoulders settled. "I got to get back." He turned to go.

She grabbed his arm. Kissed his cheek. "Thank you, my friend," she whispered. "I might not be obeying, but I do hear you."

He sighed. "Guess that's the best I can hope for right now." He cast one more glare at Gamble. "The girl's got plenty of folks who'll be watching you, my man. Best do right by her."

Gamble's jaw flexed, but he nodded. "I'm trying."

Clearly unconvinced, Darrell waved and ambled off.

Leaving Jezebel staring after him as she wondered what she'd gotten herself into.

"You look amazing."

She jolted. Glanced down. "I'm barefoot," she observed.

"I noticed. Cute toes."

Her head jerked up. His face was still drawn, but he was making an effort to get past the awkwardness.

"My feet are too big to be cute."

"You have this 'big' complex, don't you?"

"Try being the girl so tall she has to stand on the back row with the boys in seventh grade...and she towers over all of them."

He grinned. "You're shorter than me."

"Not that much. Most men find that intimidating."

He snorted. "Do I look intimidated?"

She took her time scanning.

Nope. What he looked was...hot. Black slacks and black T-shirt accentuated his shaggy black hair and framed those startling blue eyes. "I guess not."

"What I am is hungry. You have shoes, right?"

"Somewhere."

His eyes warmed. "Why don't you get them, and we'll get this whatever-it-is on the road."

"Not a date," she said.

"Not yet," he answered.

Jezebel's heart knocked hard within her chest. Speechless for one of the rare times in her life, she chose to scamper inside and simply grab her shoes.

AT HIS BEST, Gamble was aware that he'd never been what anyone would consider a conversationalist; however, he found his tongue all but frozen to the top of his mouth now. Usually, Jezebel required no help summoning words; she generally had enough for both of them.

Tonight, though, the drive was silent.

"Sorry I only have this truck," he finally said.

"What?" She dragged herself from her thoughts. "Oh." She waved off his concern and smiled faintly. "I'm not a car snob." When it seemed she might fall quiet once more, she made a second effort. "My requirements from a vehicle are simply that it run and have a radio."

"What about heater? A/C?"

She shrugged. "Nope, music first. I can put on or take off clothes. Um—" She cast a sideways glance. "I mean, you know…well, I mean I didn't mean…"

For someone so dazzling, she was actually a little goofy. He grinned. "I didn't read anything into your words just because you were once a stripper."

"You could really make some sense of that?"

His smile widened. "It wouldn't be the first time you babbled around me, Jezebel." And he began to relax a little. She was talking now. Everything would work out.

"I do not babble." She faced the front and crossed her arms.

"You do. Which is strange, in and of itself, as you're the most terrifyingly resourceful, practical person I've ever met."

"I am not—" Her gaze whipped to him. "I am?"

"Yes. I can't say I like it."

"Why not?"

"Because I'm not very damn comfortable lusting after a schoolmarm."

Her eyes were lasers now. He nearly groaned. From the echoing silence, he could tell he had her full and complete attention. The atmosphere in the cab of the truck grew dense. Thick with more than he could sort out.

At last, she sniffed. "I'm hardly a schoolmarm. I'm barely educated."

"Doesn't matter. Anyway, you're as smart as anyone I've encountered."

Her jaw dropped. Then she bit her bottom lip, and he wanted to groan for a different reason.

She faced front again, then wheeled back. "Really? You see me as smart?"

"You don't?"

She stared at him for a long time. "No one has ever said that to me in my whole life," she said softly.

Inside him, warmth spread. "Doesn't mean I'm

wrong." He glanced over, to see wonder stealing across her features. "Don't you consider yourself an intelligent woman?" he repeated.

Her voice was dreamy when she answered, "I guess I do."

She fell quiet again, but now, the silence didn't feel so lonely.

THE PLACE he'd brought her to wasn't swank or fussy; it was a blues joint that happened to serve great food, as well. More than half the faces were black and more than a few were old, life's rough roads carved on their skin. She could read so much by simply watching their heads nod to the lyrics, their gnarled fingers tap out the soulful beat.

When the band took a break, she and Gamble talked. She discovered a man with a wide range of interests. He might have lived most of his years in a tiny town, but his artistic vision and, she would guess, the severity of Charlotte's health problems had given him insights beyond his age. In some ways, Gamble was an old man masquerading as a young buck... except the forces of nature and of his own body were conspiring to remind him that he was not ready for his twilight years. He was a male in his prime.

And prime he definitely was. Sitting at a small table, their chairs only inches apart, she was intensely aware of Gamble as a man. A sexual being. She had to forcibly restrain herself from leaning toward him, a moon drawn into a sun's orbit, though the gravitational forces would inevitably destroy it.

She was not in his league. He was on the verge of real fame, not a small-town boy anymore. He might have spent his earlier life certain that Three Pines held all he needed, but she had to wonder how long he would have been content, even had Charlotte lived.

Maybe his devotion to her would have kept him rooted there forever, but the fact remained that now he was a free agent, and a very talented one at that. All too soon, he would move on to the bigger stage, where he belonged.

Her fantasy might be that vine-covered cottage with babies and puppies, but he was destined for more.

He glanced at her just then and leaned nearer to whisper in her ear. "You okay?"

Was she? She had a lump in her throat for what might have been, but he'd been right when he said she was practical to her core. She summoned a smile. "Yes. The music's wonderful."

"Would you like to dance?"

She remembered their first night. First dance. What had happened next.

You're playing with fire, girl.

Probably. But I'll have memories when he's gone.
"Yes," she answered. "I believe I do."

THEIR FIRST DANCE hadn't lasted long, Gamble thought as he drew her into his arms. They'd gone from zero to hot sex with blinding speed. He planned to make this dance different.

He couldn't say exactly why they were on a date tonight, except that the longer he spent around Jezebel Hart, a woman he was so sure he'd pegged clearly at the start, the more he realized he had yet to discover about her. Her physical appearance smacked a guy in the head and left his ears ringing; it was a continuing surprise to find out what you saw on the surface was only the merest fraction of who she was.

And he was dogged by the sense that they'd gotten this whole relationship backward.

She really was, despite her protests and her past, more Victorian maiden than libertine. Maybe she had learned to use her body's stun value as a tool or a defense, even a weapon, but the inner Jezebel was, in some ways, a prude.

She was also a scrapper. And fascinating as hell.

He was hard-pressed to credit what appealed to him most. Though she, like most women, he suspected, would balk at being called sturdy, that was exactly what Jezebel was, much like his mother, now that he considered it, and Lily, too. Realizing that he didn't have to be on guard every second, after all those years of vigilance, was a huge relief, though to admit so pained him.

But that didn't mean that Jezebel was bulletproof. Her bossy manner hid a very tender heart. She deserved romance; what he'd gleaned about her earlier life told him she'd had little of it.

The mournful, bluesy notes wrapped around them, and he heard Jezebel sigh.

So he pulled her closer and let the music take over.

THE SILENCE in the truck on the way back hummed a different tune, more comfortable because they'd found much to like about each other, but also buzzing with the remembered feel of body against body, of curves brushed against angles. Palms transmitting the messages their voices feared to say.

When he stopped in front of her door, he was grateful to note the bar shut down for the night and Darrell gone. He didn't want the harsh glare of her self-appointed bodyguard to pierce the evening's soft glow.

In some ways, Gamble was more nervous than he'd ever been in his life, however absurd that might seem, given that they'd already been physically intimate with each other. That he was hardly inexperienced.

But this night was different.

For the first time since he'd been widowed, he would not simply have sex. Instead, he would make love.

For Jezebel's sake, he was intent on doing it right, but he had no idea what that meant.

The dome light flared, and he realized that she was exiting. "Wait."

When she faced him, her eyes were huge. In them, he could see how unsettled she herself felt, and her comprehension of his disquiet. Somehow, through all their missteps, they had learned some things about each other. Had become friends, yes.

But more than friends. He cared about Jezebel. He waited for the usual guilt to assault him, surprised to discover only twinges of it present.

He thought she might care about him, too, and that should make his next move easier.

It didn't.

She smiled sadly at his protracted silence. "It's okay, Gamble. Really." She slid from the seat. "I had a good time. Thank you."

"So did I." Another gaping lull in conversation.

"Maybe—"

"Don't assume—"

They'd spoken at once.

"Ladies first." He gestured to her.

She lifted one shoulder. "I was only going to

assure you that this doesn't obligate you to anything. It was a lovely evening, but I recognize that it wasn't really a date."

Unexpected anger surged. "What if I would like it to be one?"

She seemed startled. "Do you?"

He broke the connection. Stared out the windshield. Wondered.

"Right," she said. The door clicked shut faintly, and she crossed in front of the headlights. Pulled her key from her bag.

She would let him go. Would demand nothing of him because she was so damn kind and generous. Defender of the weak, champion of lost causes—

He leaped from the driver's side. Bridged the distance in a few long strides. Clasped her arm and whirled her around.

"I don't have all the answers," he growled. "I don't know what the hell to do with my life or my cottage or much else, but I am sure of one thing, Jezebel." Ruthlessly, he steadied his free hand, then tipped her chin up.

Her eyes were wet. He'd made her cry again, damn it.

Her frame shivered, but she forced it straight.

Her courage shamed him.

"I—" He swallowed. "I'm not good at words,

Jezebel, but I wish I were. For the first time in longer than I can remember, this big hole inside me isn't so huge anymore. Somehow you're responsible."

He glanced away, then back. "I refuse to be one of your charity cases, but—" He stopped, seeking a path through the jumble.

"But what?" she prompted.

He made himself to meet her gaze. "I don't want to leave tonight."

Her lashes swept down, hiding her thoughts.

Then up. "You don't have to." She held out her hand.

Gratefully, he took it. She turned. Stuck the key in the lock.

"Jezebel."

She halted.

"This is different. From before."

She nodded. "I believe you."

"I don't…I can't promise—"

She revolved, smothered his words with her fingers. "You don't have to," she whispered.

Then she replaced her fingers with her mouth in a kiss that tasted of tears and sweetness.

NOW THE SILENCE was their ally, a veil to disguise all they feared, all they longed for…all they could not say. Dared not.

Hands spoke for them, instead. Lips. Tongues

murmured no words, yet were the tender translators of a new language of uncommon grace.

By the glow of one fat candle, Gamble wooed her. Let desire flick over her skin and his like so many flames, yet each time the heat built to unbearable proportions, he smothered it, then rekindled, until their skins were slick with sweat, their fingers grasping for purchase. Their minds lost to this world and locked in their own.

Jezebel threw her head back with a moan torn from her depths. "Gamble, please..."

He denied the plea. "Not yet. Once more." Arms shaking from the effort of holding himself apart from her, fiercely intent on giving her everything in his power, he patiently began again. Stirred the embers until the fire inside them whipped into ecstasy.

Jezebel wept when at last he entered her, and moisture stung his own eyes. They clung together as though marooned from everything familiar, and the power of their joining shuddered down his spine.

And when at last there was silence again, gratitude was woven into the spaces of it.

For the first time in more years than he could count, Gamble felt warmth seep into the dead place that had been his heart.

The future was clouded but no longer choked with

despair. He still had no idea where his road would lead...but he did not tread it with leaden feet.

Jezebel's fingers danced lightly over his hair, smoothing it as if she could ease the tangles inside him. He lifted his head to tell her that she already had.

Her smile was a pretty secret, the age-old mystery known only to women, the Mona Lisa smile, Rossetti's Proserpine. Helen of Troy meets the Good Witch Glinda.

As he studied her in bemusement, she lowered her lashes, and color stained her cheeks.

He stroked that soft, creamy skin. "I admire you."

Her eyes flew open. "Why?"

"A lot of reasons, but among them your courage."

Pleasure bloomed in her gaze. "I'm not so brave."

"You are. I can only imagine what it was like for you to make your way on your own. For someone like you to bare yourself before strange men."

Joy fled. She tensed and started to roll away.

He trapped her. "No. Don't run from this. It's honest praise. Doing so must have torn pieces out of you."

She wouldn't look at him. "I tried not to let it, but—" She shoved at him and scooted across the bed.

He caught her. Brought her back. "You know why I understand?"

"How could you?"

"In New York, I had to stand there with bits of

my soul exposed under gallery lights while self-important jerks tried to tell me what my paintings meant. Had the nerve to put prices on them when they had no clue how it ripped at me to create them, how my guts lay bleeding on each canvas. That I could hardly stand to pick up a brush, because every time I did, it meant I was taking a step into life and away from—" He broke off.

"Charlotte?"

He could deny it, but there she was, the ghost in the bed.

He shoved to standing. "Yeah." His hands raked through his hair, and he began to pace as the old restlessness gripped him. "Sorry."

"Gamble?"

He paused.

She sat cross-legged in the center of the bed, the spread drawn up to cover her, drifting around her like sea foam. "I've said you can talk about her to me. I don't mind."

He was sure that she was sincere. "I've talked too much. Do you mind if I shower?"

Her face fell, and he damned himself for ruining the evening. "Sure. Go ahead."

He took a step toward her. "Just let me be by myself for a minute, and I promise—"

"I told you I don't expect anything."

He stared at her. "But you should. You're entitled."

She rose. "Maybe I'll make a pot of tea." She managed a smile. "The towels are beneath the sink, since there's no linen closet. Make yourself at home. I'll just be in the kitchen when you're done." She wrapped a sheet around herself and waited for him to give her privacy.

He owed her a lot more, but this, at least, he could do for her and not screw up, so he found his way to the bathroom and left her alone.

THE CONTRAST BETWEEN the splendor of what they'd shared and his sudden distance rattled her. Jezebel dressed in a hurry in the most sexless garments she could find, an old pair of sweatpants and a paint-stained T-shirt. Over them, she donned a sweater. Though the night wasn't chilly, she couldn't seem to get warm.

The kettle was on, the teabags waiting in mugs. Honey and sugar and cream stood ready. She actually hoped Gamble would refuse the offering and simply leave, but just in case, she hunted for a box of cookies she'd bought and stashed away.

Stashed. Oh, dear God. He was in the bathroom with—

She heard the bathroom door crash open. Through the bedroom, she saw him emerge, striding her way with a box in his hand.

Her mind refused to accept what she already knew.

"What is this?" he asked.

His face had lost all color. His eyes were hollow, his voice a rasp.

She couldn't speak, only able to stare at him with her heart a sickening thump inside her chest.

"We used a condom. Every…damn…time." He bit out each word as if it held a bitter taste. "Please tell me this is because of someone else. Someone before."

The temptation to lie to him lay sweet on her tongue. How simple it would make everything. How easy for him to go.

But after tonight, after what she'd felt with him…

"The—" She had to clear her throat. *Try again.* "The condom broke. The first night."

Pain twisted his features. "Why haven't you already performed the test?"

An absurd impulse to laugh burgeoned. There was nothing funny about any of this. "I was going to. I couldn't at first because—" She hesitated. "You have to wait until you've missed…you know."

Hope flickered. "So you're not late?"

How she wished she could give that hope breath. For both their sakes. "Not yet, but I could have done it this morning."

"So why didn't you?"

Because you came to me last night, and you let me tickle you? You giggled? You had a water fight with me?

You said you'd let me rent your cottage?

He didn't look like a man who wanted to be reminded of the fun they'd had together. The person in front of her was the angry stranger who'd ordered her off his property and told her she wasn't fit to wipe her shoes on Charlotte's mat.

She settled for another truth. "I was afraid."

A mixture of emotions skipped over his face. He scrubbed them away with one hand.

Then tossed the box at her. "Do it now." Not a suggestion.

The kit fell to the floor at her feet. "Now?" she repeated like a half-wit. Fear grabbed her in a merciless fist.

"Now."

"But what— I don't know what to do if—" She stumbled over the words.

"Neither do I." His jaw flexed. "Go on, Jezebel. Get it over with."

The man who'd made such tender, sweet love to her had disappeared as completely as if he'd never existed.

She could refuse, but she had a sense that he'd stand over her and make sure if that was required.

But it was a quiet, haunted ripple through his expression that altered the balance.

Reminded her that he had as much to lose as she did.

Sour sickness rose in her throat for all that she'd forfeited, for no matter the test results, Gamble would never trust her again, wouldn't play with her or woo her as he had only moments before.

She would like to blame Charlotte, but the truth was that he'd never been hers to keep anyway. She'd been a realist all her life until she'd met Gamble Smith; then his pain had spoken to her, and she'd faltered. Had begun wishing only to help a lonely man and wound up falling in love with him, even though he had been clear from the first that his heart was not available.

Some people just aren't meant for those ivy-covered cottages, Jez. You ignored that at your peril.

She hadn't been sure how she'd react to whatever the test kit told her, but she'd expected to be able to deal with it alone, at least.

It seemed that even privacy was too much to ask of the hateful creature called Fate.

She bent and picked up the box just as the teakettle whistled.

"I'll shut it off," Gamble said.

And walked a wide arc to keep from coming near her.

SHE FUMBLED THE BOX and spilled its contents to the floor. She wanted to scream or throw something, to melt away into a place where she didn't have to feel this nasty mix of humiliation and sick nerves.

The situation should have been different. If she'd imagined this moment, she would have cast it as one of ceremony and reverence, of the heart-stopping, life-changing instant when she would greet the knowledge of her child's existence…or grieve alone for what would not be.

Instead, this was to be a duel, a confrontation. No span of seconds to let her heart soar or her tears flow, to spin fantasies of the life she and her baby would share or mourn for the one that had slipped away.

In that instant, Jezebel got mad. She wrenched open the bathroom door and stalked toward the kitchen, primed to tell Gamble that she would do this on her own time and tell him when she was ready, but—

His head rose, and his face was ravaged.

Before her was a man with an enormous capacity for love. Just because he didn't choose to share it with her did not mean he would not care deeply for his child.

As he began to stand, she held up a hand. "I haven't begun yet." She filled her lungs with air that seemed too thin. "It just feels wrong to do it this way." She twisted her fingers together. "Is it possible you would—" She shook her head. "Never mind. I'll only be a minute."

She prayed he'd stop her. Tell her she could call him later.

A glance back showed him still staring at her, his eyes dark holes in his face.

She marched off as if to a guillotine. With hands steady enough to mock her, she performed all the steps.

While she waited, she thought she heard his footfalls and pictured him outside the bathroom door. *Can't you leave me a little space?* she longed to ask. *Just a tiny gap so I can breathe while I wait to see—*

The second pink line appeared, and despite all her sense, Jezebel uttered a small cry of excitement, quickly smothered by her hand.

But she couldn't restrain her heart, which was about to pound out of her chest. Her head felt dizzy, and her eyes swam with tears. *A baby. My baby.*

She heard a noise from the kitchen, and her throat tightened with dread.

Could she manage to lie to him convincingly? The temptation was there, certainly. His ashen face had told her all she needed to know about his reaction.

There was, of course, the obvious problem: that he would find out, whether he stayed or left.

But not if *she* left. She could start over somewhere new. Use her nest egg not for the cottage but to create a future for her baby. She would make it a bright one—work as hard as necessary, fill her days and nights with the baby's welfare, guard it and keep it safe—

An ache spread beneath her breastbone. She would miss this place, these people so much. The sense of belonging.

Then terror hit.

If she left and anything happened to her, her child would be as helpless as she'd been when she was orphaned.

No. That would not happen. Gamble could leave, and she'd give him the freedom to do so without penalty; she could take care of her child.

But she would stay. Even with no father in its life, her baby would have family beyond Jezebel herself—two uncles, an aunt and a grandmother. Whether or not they approved of Jezebel, the family Smith understood how to love; they would treasure Gamble's child. It would also be protected by a community of dear friends like Louie and Chappy and Skeeter and Darrell.

So how to make the man in the kitchen understand that she would ask nothing of him? Squaring her shoulders, she could only hope to find the words.

She opened the door to the kitchen. He was regarding it like a man facing execution.

"I thought about lying to you," she said.

"You're pregnant." His tone gave away nothing.

She couldn't quite stem the hitch in her breath. "Yes, but it's not your problem."

He blinked. "You're going to—" He cleared his throat. "Get...rid of it?"

She started to bark out *Of course not.* Instead, she coolly asked, "Do you want me to?"

He turned away, and it was all she could do not to cross the floor and force him back around so she would be able to tell what was going through his mind.

"What I do is none of your business."

"No?" He spun to face her.

"It's not your burden. I've been on my own for a long time."

"My baby is in there." He pointed to her belly, and something in his voice had her wondering if there might be hope that he cared for the child.

"I can't do this again. God—" He scrubbed at his face. Pivoted. "I need time to think." He made for the door.

"Gamble, I meant it. I'm fine on my own. I know you aren't happy about this, and I don't blame you— but I'm not Charlotte." She saw him stiffen but persevered. "I would never have tricked you."

He paused, one hand gripping the knob. "You've lied by your silence every day we've been together."

Her shoulders sank. "I could have been wrong. There was no reason to worry you."

"But you had sex with me again."

"Not sex," she whispered.

A fleeting pain crossed his features. "Just fun, you said. No strings."

You told me tonight was different. She looked at her feet. Bit her lip against the tears that threatened.

"I'm sorry—I have to go, Jezebel. I can't—"

"Fine," she answered.

"We'll talk…later. After I—"

"Get out of here, Gamble. I have thinking of my own to do."

She heard the screen door squeak.

"Don't do anything rash. Please. Just let me—"

"It's not your problem," she repeated.

And didn't look up until she heard his truck depart.

CHAPTER FIFTEEN

IT'S NOT YOUR PROBLEM.

Gamble drove without seeing, mentally staggering through a minefield of conflicting images. He couldn't sort out what had happened from the moment he'd grabbed for a towel while chastising himself for wrecking what had been an extraordinary night.

Until he'd opened the cabinet door and found the test kit.

People always said *my heart stopped* to convey a sense of drama.

He would swear his literally had. For untold seconds, he had been unable to process what his eyes registered.

Then an astonishing wave of betrayal had knocked him flat.

Still grasping for a foothold, he'd wanted her to reassure him, even as his stunned mind had recalled her admission of how long it had been since she'd last made love.

Had sex, he corrected.

There's been enough lying. You made love with her, whatever else is going on.

I was afraid. Into his memory speared her expression as she'd admitted that, pale and trembling. Transformed from the creature of light and fascination, of heart and hope, into a closed-down, wrapped-up-tight shadow of the earthy, generous woman who had opened her arms to him tonight.

And what had he said to her?

Get it over with.

Because he was shaky himself, a man who had discovered an appetite for life, at long last, but still felt a sinner for it. Wasn't it wrong to yearn for Jezebel and all she symbolized? To crave her warmth, her cheer, her indomitable strength? God help him, how different she was from Charlotte.

But it was Charlotte he loved, wasn't it? He was a one-woman man, always had been.

So now he paid. Betrayed once by fate, by the woman who was supposed to care—

He jammed on the brakes.

Echoes from past to present. Faced with a similar situation, he was behaving like some broken record.

When had he become so brittle? Such a coward?

He thought about Charlotte's stunned and grieving

face when he'd turned on her after she made her joyous announcement.

Tonight, Jezebel's vulnerability was a scrim overlaying it.

Are you going to—

Do you want me to?

He couldn't say that; out of the span of those instants of stupefied disbelief, one, quicksilver and shining, had been a pure note of fierce joy.

He'd longed to be a father before, but not at the risk of losing his wife. Fear had made him cruel.

The condom broke. Not Jezebel's fault. Not intentional.

You've lied by your silence.

But he thought he understood. She was, at heart, a nurturer and guardian. Hadn't he experienced those qualities firsthand?

I was afraid. But still she protected him. *It's not your problem.*

He blinked to attention and realized that he was near the hospital. An impulse to seek out his mother almost had him veering into the parking lot. She was the wisest person he knew, and she would give him good counsel.

But the mere thought of a grandchild would be too sweet to her. She'd never chastised him for his attitude, but he recalled how eagerly she'd anticipated that first baby, how she had been Charlotte's chief ally and ecstatic cohort as they gathered the layette he'd refused to view. Later, he'd been too absorbed in his own grief to properly comfort her when that baby was lost.

No, he would not torture his mother with the knowledge. Nor could he talk to his brothers or Lily.

He had to clear his own mind, too cluttered by reverberations of the past. That meant he would have to face the one hurdle he had approached a hundred times but balked at each occasion.

For him to do right by Jezebel, whatever that meant, he first had to paint Charlotte, for only in facing her would he be able to finally let her go.

She was past needing him, but he'd clung to her, had crawled into a hole with his memories of her and become a cave creature.

Somehow, Jezebel had looked at the pale imitation of the man he'd once been and seen something she liked. Had refused to let him seek the soothing darkness but had, instead, dragged him toward the light.

He'd let her down tonight; there were so many other ways he could have played that scene, but he'd been so caught up in the hamster wheel of his guilt and grief that he'd reacted badly.

She was innocent of blame and deserved better.

He would have to fix that. He headed his truck down the road to see if he could exorcise a ghost.

JEZEBEL COULDN'T SETTLE, so she made lists. *Find a doctor. Buy vitamins. Get a book on being pregnant. Locate a place to make my baby a nest.*

But every other item on the list was invisible: *How is Gamble? What's he thinking? Is he all right?*

In between, she paced. If only Three Pines were bigger, she could hit a bookstore. Peruse the want ads. Go to a twenty-four-hour grocery and read the labels on baby food. Comparison-shop for diapers.

Despite the disaster of the evening, though, a steady flame of joy burned within her. She might never get the cottage now, had probably lost whatever affection Gamble felt for her, definitely had a fight on her hands to find a better way to support a child.

But she was having a baby. She did a little skip. She would be someone's mother, maybe by Christmas. For a moment, visions of Christmases to come whirled like dancing maidens.

Then she sagged to the sofa, head in her hands.

She missed her mother tonight worse than anytime in her life. The woman she remembered would understand. Would be happy for her, no matter what. Would help her find her way. Grab her close and celebrate.

But she had no mother, no one to teach her the thousand and one things she desperately needed to learn in order to be the parent her baby deserved.

It was all up to her, terrified or not. She had a

chance now at her dream; the only price for this part of it was the centerpiece: the man she loved. Gamble's stricken face was never far from her thoughts.

Maybe not. Her inner optimist admonished. *You don't know.*

But she did. He would probably do the right thing by both of them and contribute to the child's care; he was a good man, after all, of that she had no doubt.

But they hadn't had time to seal the bond between them before it was sundered. Now they never would.

Talk to him. Go to him.

No. He asked to be alone.

The argument continued so loudly that at first she didn't hear the phone.

"Ms. Hart? Assistant D. A. Lansing here. I have to have you here tomorrow. I found money in the budget. Here's the number for your flight."

SEVERAL HOURS LATER, she'd lined up everything she could. Louie and Chappy would keep tabs on Skeeter; Darrell would mind the bar and feed her dog and cat. She hadn't told a soul about the pregnancy and wouldn't, not until she and Gamble agreed to make it public.

She did plan, however, to look for a book on babies at the airport, to read on the plane. And she had already found a doctor in Tyler and made an appointment for next week.

She hoped to return day after tomorrow, but the prosecutor had warned her that trials didn't always go as expected, so she packed five days' worth of clothes.

There was only one item left on her list: seek out Gamble. Maybe he wasn't ready to talk yet, but she could at least let him know she was leaving and when she would be back.

She drove by the nursery but didn't see his vehicle and wouldn't stop to ask Lily unless she had no other option. Instead, she headed for the cottage.

And there she found his truck.

But no sign of Gamble, even though she called out his name. She only had an hour left before she had to drive to Dallas.

Then she heard the music and followed it to its source.

Gamble was in the only place he'd put off-limits to her: his studio. When she neared the door, she understood why he hadn't answered her.

Music rolled out from the speakers in bountiful waves, so lush and rich with drama and heartache as to wrench tears from a stone. Now dirge, now weeping strings, swelling to a crescendo—then a voice sweet enough to tear out your heart.

And inside the music stood a Gamble she'd never met.

The artist whose mammoth talent had captivated a city full of cynics, on his face a concentration so complete that a nuclear blast would not have fazed him.

He was staring out of eyes so haunted and wounded that it was all she could do not to cry out.

Then she spotted the painting on his easel.

And Jezebel's last hope shattered.

For it was Charlotte he painted, a woman beautiful and ethereal beyond any mortal. Spun-gold hair, soft hazel eyes. Lovely and delicate as an angel's wing.

And in her lap was the child she had tried to give the man she loved more than life.

Through her tears, Jezebel smiled at the baby, chubby cheeks and tiny fists, swaddled in a blanket that seemed to be woven from a cloud.

The painting was at one and the same time the saddest, most uplifting thing she had ever seen. It wept with the love Gamble bore them both, the guilt and grief that dogged him still.

But he'd found joy there, too, and Jezebel was glad for that, even as she accepted that the price of that joy and grief was her own chance for a future with him.

She was transfixed by Gamble, by the naked emotion on his face. By the stunning power of his talent. Here was the man he was intended to be, someone much bigger than Three Pines, far beyond her small dreams.

Someone who understood love better than she ever would.

And with these realizations, she let Gamble Smith go. She would not cling or attempt to grasp more than they had shared. They would be friends, perhaps; they had experienced an intimacy that was like many of life's most precious gifts. Not meant to be captured or replicated, forced or made to stand still. Its beauty was precisely because it was ephemeral, beyond the scope of ordinary life. Impossible to pin down or make routine.

She would have a piece of him with her forever, and that would have to be enough. She would never forget him or this time they'd had together, but he was too extraordinary to try to contain.

Jezebel watched him for a second longer, even though it seemed an invasion of a communion too private to view.

Then she turned away.

And left her illusions behind.

CHAPTER SIXTEEN

IT WAS FINISHED.

Gamble stood back from the easel, within him a stillness so profound that his ears pounded with the weight of the hush.

Emerging from a painting was always like climbing to the surface after untold hours passed deep in a cavern. In the best moments, he and his art became one, his arm an extension of his mind's eye, tapping into a dark, shimmering lake. At those times, there was no Gamble Smith, no world beyond the vision that gripped him.

Sometimes the experience was misery; at its best, it was salvation.

Still inside the rim of his cave, Gamble hovered between earth and beyond, seized by a bittersweet understanding. He wanted to move on with his life, yes. Needed to. But when he fully emerged, Charlotte would truly be his past.

I'm sorry. I forgive you. I wish you could forgive me. I loved you. The boy inside me always will.

I'll never forget you.

His throat thickened. For an instant, he was tempted to go back. To retreat into the safe arms of his grief.

She needs you now.

Charlotte's voice. He'd nearly forgotten the sound of it.

He focused on the painting. Looked into the eyes he'd loved for so much of his life.

There was nothing to forgive, Gamble. You only sought to protect me.

Suddenly, the hazel eyes glowed the way they had so often, and he was reminded that Charlotte had always understood him, often better than he himself did.

He shifted his gaze to the depiction of the baby they'd lost. *Ours would have been a beautiful child, sweetheart.* Then looked back at her. *And you would have been an amazing mother.*

Inside Gamble, something eased as he, at last, talked to the woman he'd cared for since he was ten years old. He'd lost that in his mourning, the simple pleasure of conversing with her. Cut himself off from that most necessary communion.

I'll always be here to listen.

He smiled.

But you have someone else now. You're going to be just fine, Gamble.

He bowed his head as tears stung his eyes. Her voice seemed so real.

Be well, my love.

He looked up. *You, too.* He found a grin. *I hope you're running footraces up there. Dancing and leaping and...whole. Strong as you never got to be down here.*

"Gamble?"

He jolted. Lily stood at the door, worry creasing her face. Behind her was Cal, holding her hand.

Gamble blinked. "What's wrong?"

"You tell me. You've been gone since—" In the midst of crossing to him, she halted. Put her fingers over her mouth. "My God. You did it." Her voice was barely a whisper. "It's as if she could walk right out of that painting." Tears spilled over her lashes. She approached the easel, her hand out. Brushed the air over the infant's face. "Hi, baby," she murmured.

"It's absolutely stunning. Charlotte would be so proud."

He smiled. "Yeah. I think she would." And the knowledge swept through him like a cooling wind.

Lily stared. "You're all right, aren't you?"

He regarded her with surprise. "Actually, I am." His head was light and his stomach growling. He was torn between sleeping for a week and running cross-country.

But what he wished for most was to see Jezebel.

At the thought, urgency clutched him. He'd made a hash of things. He had to get to her. Tell her that he was finally free.

That she was the reason.

And he was happy about the baby.

"Lil, I have to go." He only did a cursory cleaning of his hands. All at once, nothing in the world mattered but reaching Jezebel.

"Where's the fire?"

"I have someone to find. Listen, can you run the nursery without me for a little while?"

"You mean like we already did today?"

"Huh?" He peered outside. Darkness was falling. "What time is it?"

"Nearly seven. You've been missing since last night. Cal drove by this morning, saw your truck and heard the music, so he didn't bother you, but I got worried when another night began." She took one glance back at Cal.

Cal grinned at her, and Lily blushed furiously enough to draw even Gamble's distracted notice.

"What's going on with you two?"

"Lily Belle here broke down, at long last, and went out with me last night," Cal explained. "And fell for my fatal charm."

His words were brash, but naked tenderness was

on Cal's face. And the usual tension was missing in Lily.

"You okay, Lil?" Gamble asked.

"Yeah. And Calvin is, as ever, full of hot air." But she colored again, watching him.

Gamble observed, bemused, but his thoughts kept returning to the woman he'd hurt.

Then, with obvious effort, Lily drew her attention back to her brother. "Mom will be so thrilled. That's where you're going, right?"

Gamble's mind raced ahead, wondering what Jezebel was feeling after he'd abandoned her with a test kit in her hand.

"Earth to Gamble."

He tore himself from his musing. "What? Listen, Lil, tell Mom I'll be by later. I've got to talk to someone else first."

He covered the painting to protect it, then charged out the door, leaving his sister and the man who, it seemed, had captured her at last, gaping after him.

IN THE END, though, Gamble made a hasty detour to his mother's house, showered, shaved and dressed. He spent too much time in the greenhouse, debating over what flowers to bring to Jezebel to begin his apology for the way he'd left her. Dread skated down his spine as he contemplated, then discarded, word after word. Argument after argument.

Her face rose in his mind, lit by purpose, alive with optimism that appeared to override his complete lack of welcome for her news. *It's not your burden. I'm fine on my own.*

He didn't doubt that.

But he needed her. Freed from the weight of his guilt, from the constant crowding of sorrow that had filled every inch inside him, he felt both years younger and light of heart in a manner he had never before experienced. The world seemed full of possibilities.

The one he wanted most was Jezebel.

And the child she carried inside her. His child.

For a small, still moment, he murmured to the one he had lost. *I'm sorry. It was never you. My fear ruled me. I couldn't see past it, couldn't breathe for the thought of losing Charlotte.*

But Charlotte, he saw now, had only been on loan to him, too frail to survive a lifetime together. He would have to live with his regret for squandering their last months.

Too rushed to make a decision, he grabbed a rosebush, some daylilies and an azalea, all peace offerings he would plant at Jezebel's new cottage.

Their cottage, if he had anything to say about it.

And charged into the night to find her.

SHE WAS GONE. Vanished into thin air. Darrell knew something, Gamble suspected. He was not, however, sharing or planning to share.

"You just get on back to New York City. I can't say exactly what you did to her, but I recognize a broken heart when I see one. That woman is too fine for the likes of you. Don't care how many write-ups you get. They can call you genius in every paper on earth. It don't change what you done to that girl."

Gamble had no defense to offer. Apparently, Jezebel hadn't revealed her pregnancy yet, but this was not the audience to appreciate what a shock the news had been for him, how it had thrown him. Persona non grata, he was. Even Chappy wouldn't meet his eye.

He couldn't blame them. He left the bar, its abrupt silence brimming with hostility. He walked around behind the building. Scanned the surroundings, every inch of them painted with memories. Jezebel laughing, tickling. Moaning, sighing.

Crying.

Then, from inside, he heard Rufus's whimper.

Rufus. He brightened. She wouldn't leave the dog for good.

He placed one hand on the knob, tempted to go

inside if it was unlocked and seek comfort in her belongings.

Except a sudden vision of her face intervened, tight with strain as he demanded that she forgo her privacy and—

Get it over with.

What a bastard he was. Too caught up in his own pain to notice hers. To recognize how violated she must have felt.

He withdrew his hand, dropped his forehead to the wall. He would violate her no more.

At least she was coming back.

Then a stark fear seized him. Why had she left? To get rid of the child he was so clearly unready to accept?

Do you want me to?

No. Oh, Jezebel, no. Please.

It's not your business what I do.

But it is. You can't—

I always swore that one day I'd have a real house with a white picket fence and babies and puppies and kittens.

Some of his tension eased. This was Jezebel, after all. Saint of strays. Defender of the weak.

Maker of families, however unconventional.

Still, he would not draw a deep breath until he could speak to her, make her see that he—

His eyes popped wide.

Loved her.

He paused, tried the idea on for size. Found in it a rightness that resonated clear to his bones. Gamble Smith loved Jezebel Hart, all of her, not just her stunning body but her sweetness, her bounteous heart. Her spunk in standing up to a world that had knocked her down again and again.

Her stubborn insistence on believing the best in people when so many of them—himself foremost—showed her so much less.

Sweet mercy, that was Jezebel's appearance in his life. A mercy he hadn't earned, but granted to him nonetheless, despite all his mistakes.

He'd been itching to leave since the moment he'd landed in town, but now he realized he wasn't going anywhere. Not until he and she could talk this out.

Still unsettled by the requirement to take it on faith that he would get another chance with her, Gamble departed, in search of the wisest person he knew, hoping she could help him stack the deck.

AFTER TALKING TO HIS MOTHER, he painted the rest of the night, using acrylics so they'd dry faster, but promising himself to render this image in oils with his very next effort. Oils were the only way to do her vivacity true justice.

He'd asked his mother to keep their talk in confidence, not ready yet to share with his siblings the mess he'd made, not until he had a chance to work things out with Jezebel.

Once more, his stomach jittered. He had a fleeting thought that he should call Kat, so that she could enjoy him getting his just deserts.

But he would prevail in the end, he resolved. Jezebel had every right to be furious with him; she could ignore him or rain down curses on his head. She was entitled to make him suffer.

But he had the ace in the hole: the cottage. And he would win.

He secured Lily's indulgence to manage the morning without him only by promising that she would be the first to hear why. He left her and Cal grinning at each other like a couple of kids. At some point, he'd be asking hard questions, but for now, all he could think about was Jezebel. Somehow, he'd passed beyond the need for sleep and food, fircd by an energy unlike any he'd felt before.

Hours later, the stage was set.

And now, he must wait. But if she didn't return soon, he would haunt Darrell and Skeeter until they caved.

JEZEBEL'S FEET were dragging as she emerged from her car. Two days spent waiting for nothing; she had not been required to testify, but Russ Bollinger had still been convicted. She couldn't help being relieved that he wouldn't be able to blame his conviction on her, and she could put that chapter behind her.

Home free, at last.

She stopped dead before her doorway.

But...where was home for her now?

Every hour away from Three Pines, she'd alternated between resolve and despair. She didn't have to leave Three Pines; Gamble surely would be gone the instant his mother's situation cleared.

But soon, her secret would be out, and too many people had seen them together. She'd made her peace with the knowledge that she and Gamble had no future. What worried her most was having her child suffer the consequences of having no father, if he didn't want to be involved even to the degree of claiming his child. She was familiar with being a misfit, and she would do everything in her power to save her child from the misery of it.

If she went somewhere else, she could call herself a widow and her baby would never have to know, until the time was right, that its father had made a choice. But she kept returning to the fact that if she left Three Pines, the fate she feared most for her child could materialize. The child would be defenseless, as Jezebel had once been, should something happen to her.

She'd had very little sleep since she had walked

away from Gamble's studio like a zombie. When she tried, the portrait of Charlotte haunted her...mocked her, with its reminder of a love Jezebel could never have. Tired to the bone, she unlocked the door to her makeshift quarters—

And was swallowed up in the abundant affection of one sloppy dog and the irritation of a too-long-ignored cat.

"Oh, Rufus..." For the first time since her hopes had shattered forever, Jezebel allowed herself to weep. She buried her face in his fur and clung as sobs refused to be stemmed.

She slipped from kneeling to sitting and cried out her misery, all the lost illusions, every last unattainable dream. Oscar prowled and rubbed as if to comfort her, and Rufus snuffled at her hair.

Finally, the storm abated. Drained by the force of it, she sat on the floor, hunched over, stroking her two best friends, and reminded herself of all she had to be grateful for. Eyes closed, she leaned her head against the door and focused on gathering herself to face a life that had, only a matter of days ago, seemed pretty wonderful.

She pulled Rufus close with one arm and placed the other hand on her belly. "We'll be all right, baby. I promise." She regarded her faithful friend. "Rufus, I'm going to need your help."

Then she smiled ruefully. *Look at you, asking for help from a dog. You are a head case, Jezebel.*

"Okay," she said. "Pity party over. Time to make plans." She got to her knees, then rose to her feet, kicked off her shoes and padded to the kitchen table to check her mail.

And froze.

Flowers, scattered in pots all across her kitchen counters. Roses, gardenias. Honeysuckle and azaleas.

And square in the center of the table, a note.

Jezebel, the envelope said, in bold letters.

With a tiny sketch of the cottage beside her name. One created by no other hand than Gamble Smith's.

In trembling fingers, she lifted the envelope and turned it over.

Then paused.

What could be inside it? She was terrified and thrilled, eager and reluctant.

But curiosity won. She opened the flap.

You have no reason to forgive me. I never meant to hurt you, but I realize I did. We have a lot to talk about. Please come to the cottage. I'll wait for you, however long it takes.

And signed it only *G.*

She stood there with it in her hand for a very long time, afraid to hope but desperately wishing she dared.

She thought about all she'd surmounted in her life, reminded herself that taking a simple drive to a cottage would be considered by most people to be a piece of cake, compared with stripping off your clothes for strangers or sleeping in bus stations or living alone on the streets at thirteen.

But if she'd ever been more scared, she couldn't recall it.

Because this…could be everything. Her dreams, her fantasies, a child's yearning, a woman's deepest longings.

Or it could be only a decent man trying to find a way to square accounts—

Before walking out of her life.

She squeezed the envelope—

And felt something else inside.

When she turned the envelope on its side, a key fell out. She'd seen it before, marked with a blue dot, the day Gamble unlocked the door and let her enter the house he had built with so much love.

She clutched it to her breast.

But her heart filled with sorrow. Gamble was going to leave, but conscience was making him grant her the cottage he knew she wanted so badly.

She managed a small smile. Not that long ago, she

would have been the happiest woman in the world to have the cottage for what it would mean to Skeeter and to herself. She just hadn't understood then that the man who owned it would mean so much more.

Jezebel squared her shoulders. "Okay. All right." Time to count blessings, not to mourn what she couldn't have. She glanced at the flowers, inhaled their perfume. Peered down at Rufus. "Want to come with me, fella?" She could use the reinforcements.

In the end, though, she decided she had to face Gamble alone. She petted Rufus and Oscar, grabbed her purse—

And left to get this—whatever it was—over with.

EACH REVOLUTION of her tires brought a memory, and Jezebel stopped fighting them. Someday, she would share them—the G-rated ones, anyway—with his child.

At last, the cottage emerged into view, and she fell still before the onslaught of emotions rolling over her.

Everywhere she looked, she saw him. Angry and demanding that she go. Sweaty and gorgeous, hacking at vines. Wet and muddy, wrestling with Rufus. Pain-racked and haunted as he waited while she went inside.

And caught in the spell as he painted a masterpiece of the woman who was his life.

When she stopped the car and emerged, he was nowhere to be found after all. She walked to the front door on unsteady legs, with each step attempting to imagine living here with her child.

His child.

On the front porch, she stalled, overwhelmed by longing. Trying not to wish for a miracle. Unable to succeed.

Finally, she opened the screen door, slipped the key into the lock and turned. Entered a house that would, she feared, forever be Charlotte's and never hers.

But love dwelled here, and she would add to its account. Swell its coffers every day so that the baby inside her would never experience what it felt like to be abandoned or alone.

She glanced automatically toward the mantel, where his magnificent painting of the cottage last hung—

And halted in shock.

For there, against the stone, was a new painting.

Of her. The sketch she still treasured, of her in the filmy gown, rendered in paints this time. Exploding with life and color, rich bronze and burgundy background, her hair raven black, her gown the green of her eyes.

"You made me beautiful," she murmured, and stepped close.

"I only painted what I saw."

She gasped. Whirled.

And there he stood, the man who owned her heart.

For endless moments, they studied each other in silence.

Then spoke at the same time.

"You're beautiful—"

"I know you're leaving—"

He frowned. "You do?"

Her spirits sank to her toes, but she squared her shoulders and refused to let that show. "Of course. Your life is in New York. You have a bright future ahead. You're too talented to bury yourself here in East Texas."

Gamble was still feeling the jolt of her presence, so he was slow to argue. However much he thought he'd done her justice in the portrait, even without oils, he now understood he had failed completely. Life burst from her, glowed from every pore. Inside her dwelled an endless well of goodness, a soul so vibrant and rich with compassion and strength that his own dead heart had stirred and stretched toward her as a seedling seeks the light.

The nerves that had plagued him as he waited for her were still on edge about her reaction to all he'd done—

But deep within him, impatience demanded that he stop sitting on the sidelines of life and leap back into the fray.

"What about you, Jezebel? What's your future?" He walked closer. "Where will it play out?"

"Me?" Her eyes darted to the side. "Oh, well, I…"

He'd never seen her flustered. Hope rose in him. She didn't have everything figured out. "Surely the woman who bosses everyone else around has some idea what she wants for herself."

He moved in on her. She took a nervous step to the side.

He captured her, unable to stand not touching her for one more second. But as he pulled her near, she resisted. "Jezebel?"

Her head was down. He tipped up her chin. "Honey, what's wrong?"

The eyes that beheld him were huge and green… and swimming with tears. "You know what I want," she whispered. "Don't tease me with what can't happen. I realize that you and Charlotte had something special. I understand that you'll never get over her. I just wish—" She pressed her lips together to stem the words.

"What?" he asked softly, sensing that he must tread carefully.

Only silence greeted him, at once intimate and immense, as if the slightest step wrong would destroy what was so fragile between them.

Gamble was not a man to discuss his emotions.

No guy liked it, and he preferred not to even think about them, much less voice them.

But for the sake of this beautiful soul, he would try.

He released her while he gathered his thoughts. Jezebel visibly shrank into herself, and he sought to explain. "It's not—" He cleared his throat. "Oh, hell. I told you I'm lousy with words."

He could divine nothing from her brief nod, and she had resumed staring at the floor.

"I love Charlotte," he began. She flinched, but he made himself forge on. "I always will. She and I were bound from the time I was ten and she was eight. I felt responsible for her. She was always frail." Every sentence seemed to make Jezebel feel worse, but he wouldn't lie to her.

"I was angry about her being pregnant, but I don't have anything against babies. My reaction was more about how scared I was of losing her. I wanted to be a father. I still do."

Jezebel's gaze shot to his, and he saw an instant of wild hope before she quickly shuttered it. "So—" Her voice was hoarse. "You…might be willing to acknowledge this child, even if—" She bit her lip. "I mean, you'll leave, and I can raise this baby fine by myself, but—"

"So you didn't—" He halted. Closed his eyes. "The baby's safe."

"Of course. I never considered not keeping it."

"I'm glad."

"You are?"

She was so stunned that anger got the better of him. "Of course I am, damn it."

She opened her mouth automatically. "That's a—"

"Dollar," he finished for her. And fell the rest of the way into love. "I'll put the money in your bleeping jar."

"I'm sorry. You don't have to."

He couldn't stay away from her anymore. Had to touch her again. "Jezebel, why is it you'll fight for everyone else but yourself? Would you honestly just let me waltz back to New York so easily? Demand so little of me?"

Her pupils nearly swallowed the green. "You love Charlotte, not me. I'm a realist. That sort of devotion doesn't happen twice in a lifetime. I don't expect it to."

"Then you're selling yourself too short, and it makes me so—" He inhaled, then abandoned caution. "Damn mad. Go ahead. Fine me again."

A small smile played around her lips, but her eyes were an aching tangle of longing and resignation.

"I can't forget Charlotte, no." When Jezebel averted her face, he brought it right back. "She's a part of me. My life with her made me who I am. But she's my past. That won't grow or change, yet I will. I have, already, because of you."

He felt his words vibrate through her, and that beautiful, too-honest face let her yearning show through, speckled as it was with caution he understood was squarely his fault.

So he redoubled his efforts. "I love you, Jezebel Hart. I want a chance with you. A life with you."

She blinked. "But what about your career and New York and—"

He smiled. Shook her gently. "Don't you get it? I'm not going back there. I can paint anywhere. I'll have to visit for shows, but you can go with me, you and—"

He glanced down. Extended his hand toward her belly, then paused. "May I?"

She bit her lower lip and nodded.

He touched her. Felt the warmth of her still-flat belly. Cupped his fingers as if to cradle the new life.

When she tenderly placed her own hand over his, he could truly breathe for the first time in days. Months.

Years, really.

"You're so strong," he marveled. "For years, I've had to be…careful." He refrained from bringing up Charlotte's name. "But I need you to believe that you can lean on me. You're not alone now."

A jumble of emotions swept over her face, among them wonder and more than a little reluctance. She opened her mouth, then hesitated.

"What?"

"You said that you can't live here."

"I didn't believe I could." It was time to face the last hurdle. Prove to her that he was committed. "Come with me."

"Where?"

He didn't answer; instead, he led her down the hall, clutching her hand.

Doubts rushed in. He wheeled in front of a door. "Never mind. Maybe I shouldn't have—"

Her brow wrinkled. "What's in there?"

He ranged himself before the opening, all faith in his bright idea vanished. "I have no idea what I was thinking," he muttered.

She reached for the knob.

"No, don't— You—"

Too late. She'd opened the door.

Jezebel gasped at the sight.

"I meant well, I swear it." He tugged at her arm. "Stand back, and I'll get rid of it."

Jezebel barely breathed as she absorbed the sight of walls covered with stunning paintings of nursery rhymes, executed not in pastels but in bold, glowing colors, obviously the work of the man at her side.

She was speechless at the beauty of it.

"Oh, Gamble…"

Then she realized that the room was empty of furniture, except—

A crib. So sturdy and graceful…from the tension in the man beside her, she was sure it was the one he'd made for Charlotte. She covered her mouth with her free hand.

"I knew it. Wrong thing to do. I'm an idiot. Of course you wouldn't be comfortable with anything that had to do with Charlotte or—"

All she could do was shake her head at first, as the room and the crib blurred in her vision.

He strode across the room and grabbed one end. "Go back in the living room. I'll disassemble it."

She leaped toward him. Stilled his hand. Stroked the satiny wood. "No," she finally managed. She gripped his fingers. "It's the one, isn't it? The crib you brought home that day?"

He nodded, his expression miserable. "You'd be worried. I should have seen that. Be afraid that something would—" His gaze shifted to her belly. "Wait outside."

She cupped his face. "You fashioned this with your own hands. With love in your heart." She gestured to the walls. "Painted these. Priceless, all of it."

"You're not superstitious?"

She shook her head. "Over the years, I've learned that you make your own luck. Bad things happen, but you just…deal with them." She smiled. "It's only between us, Gamble, how to deal with your past. To honor Charlotte's memory this way might be odd to some, but to me, it feels…right. We knit two parts of your life together."

The tension in his frame eased. His voice was thick when he spoke. "I swear that heart of yours is as big as the world. I'm not a good man, Jezebel, but I want to be one for you. Will you let me give you a home? Make a family with me?"

They stood there, mere inches apart, the moment ripe with words and dreams and fears and hopes.

"I would love nothing more." Jezebel's throat brimmed with tears. "But you're wrong. You are a good man, Gamble Smith."

He sagged as if with great exhaustion. She rose to her toes and wrapped him in her arms, while his slid around her waist. Slowly, they rocked together, gathering to themselves what had so nearly been lost.

Gamble turned his face into her hair and whispered into her ear, "Babies and puppies and kittens, right?"

She laughed shakily. Gratefully. "Maybe even horses and chickens."

His mouth curved in a grin. "And every last stray, animal or human, who crosses your path, I'm damn sure."

She leaned back and drank in the sight of him. "That's four dollars for the jar."

"What if I don't have it on me?" His eyes took on a twinkle. "Will you take payment in kisses?"

"I think something can be arranged." She was smiling as his head dipped, and his lips brushed hers.

"But don't you dare tell Louie."

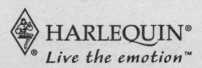

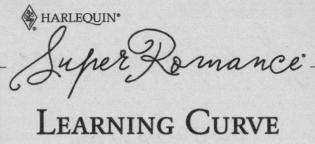

LEARNING CURVE

by Terry McLaughlin

(HSR #1348)

**A brand-new Superromance
author makes her debut in 2006!**

Disillusioned high school history teacher
Joe Wisniewski is in a rut so deep he's
considering retirement. The last thing he wants
is to mentor some starry-eyed newcomer, so
when he gets an unexpected assignment—
Emily Sullivan, a student teacher with a
steamroller smile and dynamite legs—
he digs in deeper and ducks for cover.

On sale May 2006
Available wherever Harlequin books are sold!

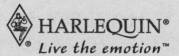

HARLEQUIN®
Live the emotion™